The Secret Journal of
Ichabod Crane

CRANE

The Secret Journal of
Ichabod Crane

Alex Irvine

THREE RIVERS PRESS
NEW YORK

Published in the United States by Three Rivers Press,
an imprint of the Crown Publishing Group,
a division of Random House LLC, a
Penguin Random House Company, New York.
www.crownpublishing.com

Three Rivers Press and the Tugboat design are registered
trademarks of Random House LLC.

Library of Congress Cataloging-in-Publication Data
Irvine, Alexander (Alexander C.)
    The secret journal of Ichabod Crane / Alex Irvine. — First edition.
    1. Sleepy Hollow (Television program : 2013–) 2. Diary fiction.
I. Irving, Washington, 1783–1859. Legend of Sleepy Hollow. II. Title.
    PN1992.77.S6125I78 2014
    791.45'72—dc23   2014030654

ISBN 978-0-553-41898-9
eBook ISBN 978-0-553-41899-6
5578 7609 9/14
PRINTED IN THE UNITED STATES OF AMERICA

Book design by Elizabeth Rendfleisch and Anna Thompson
Cover design by Gabriel Levine
Cover photograph ©Twentieth Century Fox Film Corporation
Illustrations on pages 21, 22, 39, 62, 93, 122, 140, 144, 147, 175, 185, and 190 by
John Burgoyne.

10 9 8 7 6 5 4 3 2 1

First Edition

The Secret Journal of
Ichabod Crane

One scarcely knows where to start. To commit the facts to writing—if facts indeed they are, and not the last failing sparks of a soul being freed from its mortal confines—is to begin to believe them. Dare I?

I must.

I am Ichabod Crane, born in the year 1749 in the city of London in England. I came to the New World in 1770 and followed the dictates of my conscience to the side of the colonial rebels in 1771.

It seems this is the year 2013 Anno Domini, and I have been given new life—how, I know not; why, I know not. I am in a cell, lit harshly by lamps that appear to be hidden behind glass panels set in the ceiling. The table is made of an unusual stonelike substance; so too the chair. There is little wood in evidence and some of the furniture appears to have steel legs. What people are these, who can spare steel for the legs of chairs?

They believe me a murderer and are not reticent with their accusations. Yet they have treated me humanely, in marked contrast to the few interrogations I experienced at the hands of the British over the past year—or the past two hundred thirty-two years? Surely it is still 1781 and this is a dream? Or I have died, and the afterlife is far different than any man might have supposed . . . cold, as if all the natural odors and moistures of the air have been removed. Like the air a machine might breathe.

It has been some hours now. The sounds of the language here are quite strange. Vowels are flat, phrasings staccato and very fast. This is not the language of angels. Therefore I live—unless this be the infernal realms! Surely not. My life has had a full complement of ordinary sins, but I have endeavored always to do what was right. Also, I cannot credit the idea that hell itself would be so cold and impersonal.

Well, I am no revenant. Rather than the scent of decay, my nostrils are full of some damnable perfume worn by one of the constabulary. Frightful. All that remains is to believe I am alive. Alive again! Yet how?

I am accused of horrific crimes, and I have refused to admit anything. The men I have killed knew the side they had chosen. I appealed to these authorities to contact General Washington, and they responded with astonishment, some with open ridicule. They even dared question my name—as if they had never heard of a man named Ichabod!

Gather your head, Crane. You have been in unusual circumstances before, and you survived by keeping your wits . . .

I will discern the truth—if, that is, I can keep my head.

———

At least they have permitted me to write, though if they take this journal from me it will do nothing to alter their belief that I am insane. Yet I will hold nothing back. I have always used my journals to collect private thoughts that have yet to take their full shape; reminiscences, drawings, and documents that may prove useful later; and any other bits of flotsam that wish to escape my mind onto their pages.

The act of writing, through its peculiar alchemy whereby the fruits of the mind are transformed into symbols intelligible to all literate minds—this is the greatest magic, perhaps. It is without doubt the greatest tonic for the sanity of a man such as myself, displaced two centuries and given the dark gift of life after death. I am a revenant in a time not my own, and also it seems a soldier in a war of whose many fronts I had no inkling—before today.

I have told my story to the constabulary but will set it down again here, because during the course of my interrogation I learned as much from their questions as they did from my answers, or more. The Hessian mercenary I struck down in 1781 lives again. It can be no coincidence that I was returned to my senses at the same time. I shot him from his horse scant miles from where I now sit, the ball clearly striking him in the breast—but he rose again and dealt me a mortal wound with his axe. With the last of my strength I returned his blow, separating his masked and tattooed head from his shoulders. After that, I remember very little. At triage my wife's face—oh, Katrina, what became of you in the years after my passing?—was the last I saw until I emerged from my sleep in a riverside cave.

The supernatural life given the Hessian surely explains why General Washington ordered me to seek and kill any man with the figure of a bow tattooed or scarified on his hand. That symbol bears investigating, if I am ever to be permitted my freedom.

They have a machine that can distinguish truth from lies by means of electrical signals transmitted along the skin. What would Benjamin Franklin have made of this odd descendant of the key dangling from his kite string? For that matter, of the electrical light that shines in every room of every building, and from fixtures within the horseless carriages they call cars?

Despite the machine's support of my tale, they have determined me fit for the asylum. One hopes the masters of that Bedlam will forbid cloying perfumes. Regardless, I hope to be able to keep this journal there. Already it has proven a great comfort.

There is another, more practical and pessimistic reason to record my experience. If I do not survive my battle with the Hessian, others will step into my place. For those successors (though I hope they succeed me none too soon!) I write this journal, that it may assist them in navigating the thickets of superstition, spycraft, and malevolence—and the Infinite alone knows what else—that oppose us. My role in the colonies' rebellion taught me that the most important actions of a war take place on unnamed battlefields. This may be one of those, and I may die on it; but if I must die, I would not have all I know perish with the extinguishing of those final sparks of my brain.

I am afraid, and unashamed of my fear. Only the fool shows no fear when he fights for his life against an opponent such as the one we face, and only a fool is unafraid when thrust into a situation utterly foreign, alone.

This is truly a fantastical future into which I have emerged. Chattel slavery is a thing of the past, and distant enough in fact that Abigail Mills, a black (or African-American, as I have learned is another nomenclature of this era) sheriff's deputy, treated my disbelief as a joke. Perhaps this is part and parcel of her belief that I am mad, or perhaps she humors me in an effort to draw from me an admission of guilt in the decapitation of her sheriff. This mixing of races and peoples is evidently taken for granted in the—to write these words!—United States of America.

I must correct myself. She is no deputy, but a lieutenant in what appears to be a much better organized constabulary than any known in the colonies during my time. When I learned this, and addressed her by her rank, she laughed; apparently these Americans pronounce the word "loo-tenant." A practical people. After all, why should the English language be beholden to bygone relics of French origin? Yet I must confess I still prefer "lef-tenant."

Whatever their pronunciation, how far they have come, that African-Americans occupy executive authority without remark.

All men are created equal, Jefferson wrote—this America strives to live that ideal. Doubtless it falls short, as do all human actions when compared against ideal goals. However, when I consider the oppression I witnessed during my time in the colonies, I cannot help but feel pride that I contributed—in whatever slight fashion—to the liberation of the colonies, which over time led to the liberation of the slaves. And Abigail's friend and colleague Brooks bears the traces of yet another history: that of the Asian peoples finding their way to these shores. Of that I know little, but hope to investigate more thoroughly.

I feel foolish now for congratulating Abigail on her emancipation. Whether I will work up the nerve to confess my foolishness, now . . . that is another matter entirely.

Regardless, Abigail is a young woman of considerable fortitude, whatever her pigmentation. She also possesses a quick wit. "You keep running your fingers over that tabletop like you're trying to pet it," she remarked. "Never seen a table before?" I could not but laugh, for I had indeed been doing exactly that, seeking to discern by touch of what substance the table might be composed. A pet table! But soon enough we returned to the drier topics of my interrogation.

She does not believe me, not yet, but she is of a most pragmatic cast of mind. If I can contribute to her pursuit of a criminal—a figure whom she considers a criminal but I know to be something much worse—she will hear me out. It must be even more difficult for her. She clings to the rational, to her belief in only the provable world of the senses. This, I believe, is why she intends to enter an advanced program of education in what they call "profiling." I gather it is a systematized means of using the evidence of a crime to deduce specifics about the unknown criminal, and thereby speed his capture.

But only a woman fleeing from the inexplicable would seize so desperately on the tangible to the exclusion of all else. There is more to the young lieutenant than she has yet spoken of, or I discerned.

And I looked, and behold a pale horse: and his name that sat on him was Death, and Hell followed with him. And power was given unto them over the fourth part of the earth, to kill with sword, and with hunger, and with death, and with the beasts of the earth.

The eighth verse of the sixth chapter of the Revelation of Saint John the Divine. This verse will not leave my mind. It was marked in the Bible that lay on my breast while I was in my sleep, a most precious book that once belonged to George Washington. I have no memory of how it came to be in my possession, although I knew General Washington well and suspect one of our allies in the war against evil must have placed it there during my slumber. The general and I met frequently throughout the years of the rebellion, and I told Lieutenant Mills of one such meeting. Since she already believes me to be a lunatic murderer, no further harm was possible, I judged, from explaining to her that General Washington himself gave me the Bible, and told me that the American war for independence was something much greater than the struggle of restive colonies yearning for self-determination. No, it was a war between the forces of light and dark—a framing I understood to be metaphorical. That war may have taken a hiatus since the Hessian and I fell together in battle in 1781, but it is now brewing once more—and hurtling toward a conclusion upon which much more than the fate of one nation depends.

For this notation can only signify that the Hessian, risen again into decapitated life, is the Horseman of Death. The first of the Four Horsemen of the Apocalypse rides in Sleepy Hollow, in the state of New York, in the year 2013. Did General Washington know this, when he sent me after him in 1781?

My perceptions of those times are somewhat scrambled. This is highly unusual due to the typical accuracy of my memory. Has my long slumber compromised my faculties?

Or is there a darker force at work?

My power of recollection has always been one of my keenest weapons. I hope it has not been dulled by disuse.

[October 5]

I am no Daniel, to interpret the dreams of kings, but I have had a dream that either confirms my madness or strengthens my inkling of the infernal link between my life and that of the Hessian. I dreamed of Katrina. My love. Yesterday I was led to her gravestone, here in Sleepy Hollow, and learned of her agonized end on the stake. The devastation this caused me is beyond words and I could not write of it then. Now I know I do not have to, for events perhaps yet more tragic have revealed her death to be a ruse perpetrated by parties yet unknown.

I say I dreamed of her, but it would be more accurate to say that she came to me in a dream. The same falcon that led me to her stone drew me through the world of this dream into a mirror world, a trackless forest wilderness where my wife appeared and revealed to me that the Hessian—the Horseman—and I were magically linked by the intermingling of our blood on the battlefield. She had prevented my death by working a spell that held me on the border between life and death. The Hessian's body was

chained and sunk in the Hudson, and we remained in our deathless suspension until he returned and I was awakened by the bond
of blood. I am the First Witness, she said . . . but to what, I do not
know—no, of course I do. Was I not just reading passages from
Revelation?

> And I will give power unto my two witnesses, and they
> shall prophesy a thousand two hundred and threescore
> days, clothed in sackcloth. These are the two olive trees,
> and the two candlesticks standing before the God of the
> earth. And if any man will hurt them, fire proceedeth
> out of their mouth, and devoureth their enemies: and
> if any man will hurt them, he must in this manner be
> killed. These have power to shut heaven, that it rain not
> in the days of their prophecy: and have power over wa-
> ters to turn them to blood, and to smite the earth with
> all plagues, as often as they will.

Quite exhilarating, the prospect of breathing fire and smiting
the earth, and so forth . . . yet all the same I would surrender those
fanciful powers for the touch of Katrina's hand, here in this world
rather than in the diaphanous fantasy of a dream. Too, the passage
goes on to speak of the circumstances of the Witnesses' deaths,
which makes being a Witness a somewhat equivocal blessing.

Still, if Witness I must be, then Witness I will be. Perhaps
General Washington knew more then he was telling me when
he made his remarks about the true stakes of the war in the colonies . . .

I have also learned that the light of the sun weakens the Horseman, but even that attenuation will not save us if he is able to recover his head. That is my next task, to convince Lieutenant Mills

that we must take possession of it. What we do with it is another question. Shall we keep it, to ensure he does not recover it? Can it be destroyed? What would happen if it were to be destroyed? We must not act rashly.

I also must free Katrina from her forest prison.

A demon, the guardian of this realm or perhaps its henchman, interrupted us then, but I know where the Horseman's head lies—beneath Katrina's headstone. I also know that the man I saw on the way to the cave was one Reverend Knapp.

Either I have seen him before or the Knapp I knew in the years of the Revolution has engendered a doppelgänger. Knapp was an ally of General Washington's subterfuges, and a stout opponent of the Crown. Confidant to the inner circle of revolutionaries, he was indispensable to our battle then. He may have recognized me as well, and wished to remain discreet—yet I must ascertain the truth of this matter without delay.

We have fought the Horseman—and at least for today, we have emerged victorious. He fell upon us as we dug up his head, and he was aided by a most unwelcome ally: the police officer Brooks, who seems to have returned from the dead. (This is apparently becoming quite a popular pastime here in Sleepy Hollow.) Only the rising sun forestalled a much gloomier conclusion to the night's events. Katrina was right; the Horseman indeed abhors the light of day. This is a weapon we must not fail to use.

I believe I understand why this Reverend Knapp—who I am sad to say fell victim to the Hessian the night before last, before I could communicate with him and partake of what must have been an invaluable store of knowledge—left the Bible in my possession, for surely he must have? Katrina would not have had it, and would have been gone from this world before Washington's own death. A mystery. One way or another, by some hand the Bible was placed on my breast, and now I have it to guide me. The Book of Revelation speaks of two Witnesses who will rise to the defense of humanity during the period of tribulation that heralds Judgment Day. If I am the First Witness, as Katrina said, who can the second be but Abigail Mills? She has expressed a kind of faith in me that leads me to believe we are bound together in a way—not the way the Hessian and I are bound, but by a higher, nobler purpose.

For Abigail has also seen the evil we are fighting—when she was a girl, with her sister. She unburdened herself about this to me, and I now understand more clearly how we are linked, bound together by our experiences. I was correct, after all, that a childhood trauma of inexplicable nature drove her to embrace the idea that only explainable things are real.

Perhaps I should attend this training in "profiling" myself. Would that I could travel at will. This world is as much wonder as terror, and I hope to see a great deal more of it. For now, though, I—and Abigail—must stop the Horseman. Now that we have his head, that unimaginable task seems to hover just on the distant border of possibility.

[October 6]

It seems that Lieutenant Mills's superiors have decided to give me the proverbial amount of rope necessary to hang myself. I am no longer housed in the asylum, which I note in passing was quite comfortable, certainly more so than some of the army encampments I endured during the former phase of my life. Now I am kept in a rooming house of sorts known as a "motel." The accommodations here are also quite satisfactory and in some cases extraordinary. In the bath, not one but two separate spigots provide water of any temperature desired, seemingly in endless amounts. I stood for quite some time in the shower and discovered that it is very easy for one's mind to wander when one is standing below a stream of hot water. It occurred to me that I had not had occasion to bathe for quite some time before the battle at which I encountered the Horseman. I gather that the people of this time bathe much more frequently than was the habit of my former contemporaries—and with all the hot water one could possibly desire, instead of buckets heated over a fire and laboriously conveyed to a washbasin, who would not?

One of the topics to which my mind continually returned was another dream, in which I entered Katrina's forest prison, what I will call Mirror World. In this dream I was fleeing the Horseman until Katrina appeared and we hid ourselves in an underground walkway. There she explained to me that my instincts regarding the passage in Revelation from General Washington's Bible were partially correct, but that I had not seen the full extent of the danger. The Horseman himself is indeed the first of the four mentioned in the Book of Revelation. He has reawakened to seek the other three and thereby bring the Apocalypse. Then she told me "one of us" was coming. I do not know what she meant by this, but I suspect an evil spirit of some sort.

Although the Horseman of Death is not the only one of his kind. The others are Conquest, or Pestilence; War; and Famine.

Did Katrina mean, perhaps, that another Horseman is coming? What else might it be?

MIRRORS.

- *Seven years' bad luck—from Roman belief that life renewed itself in seven-year cycles, and that breaking a mirror damaged the reflected person until that renewal could occur*
- *Bad luck averted by grinding fragments into dust, or burying, or immersing in running water*
- *Catoptromancy—use of mirrors for divination*
- *Jews cover mirrors during seven days of shivah, mourning for the dead—else the spirit of the departed can become trapped and prevented from moving on*
- *Chinese belief: mirrors frighten away demons due to their hatred of their own reflections*

I tried to leave the motel room but was prevented from doing so by an armed guard.

Lieutenant Mills appeared before my confrontation with the guard could escalate, and we consulted. I recounted my dream and she in turn informed me that her superior, Captain Irving, is permitting us a limited time to investigate the mysterious (in his view) events surrounding the murder of Sheriff Corbin and the death of Brooks in his cell. By some sorcery the images of his death have now been altered to remove the demonic visage we observed at first, and make it appear that he took his own life by dashing his head against the wall.

Speaking of magic, I note in passing that one of this age's incredible marvels is what they call computers. More anon; let it suffice for the moment to say how extraordinary I find it that nearly every move made by the free citizens of this republic is captured and archived by electronic means. How this universal surveillance can be reconciled with ideas of liberty I have yet to discern, yet few people here seem to think it unusual. One is put in mind of the old parable of the frog in a soup pot, put on the fire and not knowing he is being cooked because the water warms so incrementally.

Perhaps they—the ordinary citizens under such constant watch—are made to feel more secure by the astonishing advances in firearms since the musket. I have seen the personal armaments of police officers, pistols apparently capable of firing shots as quickly as the trigger can be pulled. They require no powder or wadding; these and the ball are held in a metal cartridge, discarded as the shot is discharged. With twenty of these, the Continental Army could have won the war against the Redcoats in thirty days' time. Now they ride on the hip of every police officer, and I am given to understand that all Americans save criminals and the mentally feeble may freely possess them. Long guns have also progressed. I was a fair shot with a musket in my time, but accuracy is less important now that the constabulary and the standing army may issue each member a rifle capable of firing thirty rounds in half as many seconds. Each soldier must feel himself a walking army.

Abigail decided that she would show me the archives of her mentor, the recently deceased Sheriff Corbin. As we drove to his funeral we spoke of the legend on Katrina's headstone stating that she had been burned as a witch. Knowing this was not true, I was able to speak with some distance about the trials of those women suspected of witchcraft—and of my confusion regarding Katrina's silence on the matter. She must have had a reason for not telling me. I was of course aware of the activities of a coven in Sleepy Hollow, controlled by Serilda of Abaddon and allied with the British. I suspected that Katrina's revelation must portend the

existence of another coven, and when we reached the archives my intuition was confirmed. The Sisterhood of the Radiant Heart, a white-magic coven, battled Serilda and weakened her enough that she could be tried and put to death by the magistrate Robert Daniel Furth.

However, she—like the Horseman, and like me—did not remain dead, if dead she ever truly was. Abigail took me to the scene of a murder, and I noted claw marks and the use of fire. These together with Katrina's warning in my dream confirmed for me that Serilda of Abaddon had returned to the land of the living, and though we needed no further proof, it was provided when the deceased was confirmed to be a descendant of Robert Furth. Serilda, as she was burned at the stake, swore that she would take her revenge on the magistrate's descendants and use them to return herself to life. It appears she has begun to do so.

FROM THE DESK OF
SHERIFF AUGUST CORBIN

COVENS

Coven is a variant of *covent*, *cuvent*, dates to early sixteenth century—interesting—common origin with the word *convent*. Does the etymological friendship suggest relationship between work of nuns and witches? Or suggest witches took refuge in convents? Unknown. More likely just that any group of women getting together was called by a similar word.

> Efter that tym ther vold meit bot somtymes a Coven, somtymes mor, somtymes les; bot a Grand Meitting vold be about the end of ilk Quarter. Ther is threttein persones in ilk Coeven; and ilk on of vs has an Sprit to wait wpon ws, quhan ve pleas to call wpon him. I remember not all the Spritis names . . .
> —Confession of Issobell Gowdie, Lochloy, Scotland, 1662

Thirteen is a standard number for covens. When a member dies (usually the only way of leaving; not like you can just retire), individual covens have a ritual or practice in place to bring in someone new. Strength of a coven comes from the secret held in common (we're witches!) and from the ability to work more powerful magic as a group than any individual could.

COVENS IN SLEEPY HOLLOW

Sisterhood of the Radiant Heart: I'm not sure I trust them. On the surface they seem like a bunch of do-gooders, keeping an eye on things, but they're a little too sure of themselves, like they know they're right about everything. Hints in their history about four of them who left years ago (maybe centuries?) after pulling off some big magical stunt. Trying to find out more.

Order of the Blood Moon: I know I don't trust them. They're working some bad juju. Would confront them directly, but Jennifer don't have nearly enough firepower even when J. is around. Powerful ancestor known as Serilda referred to in records—considered progenitor, mentor from afterlife—necromantic communication?

SHERIFF SLEEPY HOLLOW

**STATE OF NEW YORK
APPLICATION FOR PERMIT TO
CARRY CONCEALED FIREARMS
(Resident)**

FOR OFFICE USE ONLY	
CHECK #:_____	LICENSE #:_____
____$75.00	___$50.00 ____$10.00

____ISSUE ____DENIED   DATE:_____

___D]

SAFETY :

SEX	RACE

ZIP CODE

ZIP CODE

FIVE (5) YEARS

SDICTION. For
Portland P.D.;

OR OTHER
URISDICTION. For
f refusal.

RMITS TO CARRY
ORITY IN MAINE
rity that revoked the

Initials_____

JEAN-BAPTISTE-ALEXANDRE PAULIN, fondateur et rédacteur en chef de *l'Illustration*, décédé à Paris le 2 novembre 1859.

Early examples of a Satanic heptagram (left) and pentagram (right); Pre-Christian, with Black magic symbology.

Text from the 1587 Witchcraft Trials held in England with woodcut illustration from the period.

EARLY WITCHCRAFT HISTORY:

In anthropological terminology, a "witch" differs from a sorcerer in that they do not use physical tools or actions to curse; their maleficium is perceived as extending from some intangible inner quality, and the person may be unaware that they are a "witch," or may have been convinced of their own evil nature by the suggestion of others. This definition was pioneered in a study of central African magical beliefs by E. E. Evans-Pritchard, who cautioned that it might not correspond with normal English usage.

I have begun to feel useful in this battle. I was able to assist our cause in accessing the archives after we were denied entry into the building where they were housed. The colonial rebels built a network of tunnels below the streets of Sleepy Hollow during the early days of the war, for the transportation of men and goods. These tunnels overlapped previous subterranean chambers used for the burial of witches and were also used for the storage of munitions. I located an entry point in one of the basements of a neighboring building and we found our way into the archives.

Knowledge of the tunnels became crucial to our survival on this day, and not for the first time I had occasion to be thankful for my gift of a perfect memory. Aside: This is now apparently known as a photographic memory, but having learned the meaning of that term, I dislike it. Photographs are quite an interesting new technology, and I have collected some few—including this so-called mug shot the constabulary obtained when they detained me—for purposes of reference as well as novelty.

However, these photographs say nothing of smell or sound, and those are key elements of recollection. My memory does not consist of still images, but of experience, in all senses and with full awareness of motion and time. That fullness is absent in a photograph; I am no recording machine.

I assisted in the construction of the tunnels and remembered precisely where my cohort of rebels had left the store of munitions. Serilda too remembered the tunnels, since her bones were among those interred there. She returned to work a ritual that would make her whole again, using the ashes of Robert Furth's descendants sprinkled over her bones during the last waning of the Blood Moon, for which her dark coven was named. We confronted her and learned before her destruction that Katrina was the leader of the Radiant Heart. The explosion did not collapse the tunnels or unduly damage the buildings above. We were good craftsmen, as our Mason brotherhood demanded.

I now know that Sleepy Hollow, even by the year 1781, was the battleground where the fate of all humanity would be decided for good or ill. What else, what other specters and unholy beings, remain to be discovered? Katrina, I will have need of you. Why did you not disclose to me your powers when we still walked this earth together?

Abigail is beginning to speak to me on a friendlier basis. The depth of her feeling for Sheriff Corbin now makes more sense. He gave her a path to redemption after arresting her when she was a girl, and mentored her as she chose the path of law. Also today I made the acquaintance of one Luke Morales, a colleague of Abigail's and also her suitor. There is nothing between them now, she assured me, but I am not sure he would agree. While I am no great liar, I did manage to construct a plausible persona for Officer Morales's benefit. To those who have no need of knowing my true story, or whose reaction to learning that story I mistrust, I present myself as a history professor on leave from Oxford, where I lecture on (what is now called) the American Revolution, with a focus on treatises of civil government. This has enough of the truth to be easily remembered and presented, since I did in fact hold a chair at Merton College before abandoning it for the life of a soldier—and, later, the life of a colonial rebel. I have gone by many names during the course of my espionage, and met many of the men (and a few women) who ensured that the dream of American independence was not strangled in its cradle. Those heroes are mythic now. Their faces adorn currency and their names—Jefferson, Franklin, Washington—appear in every town, on every map. Ichabod Crane is lost to history, and that satisfies me. I do nothing for glory or renown. I do, however, wonder what the men now known as the Founding Fathers would make of the country they so tirelessly worked to create. It is a marvel . . . yet like any true marvel it must be viewed with an admixture of wonder, joy, and terror.

What, one wonders, would Jefferson think of these most unnatural events? Jefferson who once used razors and glue to construct a New Testament with all supernatural elements excised?

He might find it a grand joke played on him by the God in Whom he only halfheartedly believed . . . or, what is more likely, he would refuse to believe it at all. Although I did not know Jefferson well, I had dealings with him enough to know that he had no truck with stories of angels and demons, no matter what alleged proofs their tellers might demonstrate.

Nor would he have countenanced the true horror of taxes placed on seemingly everything under the sun. A tax on baked goods would have brought the colonists into the street even faster than the ill-fated tariff on tea. Jefferson himself might have lifted a pitchfork or a torch. Does anything remain untaxed in this world? Surely not—and all the same, the sensual pleasures of the confections known as "donut holes" are ample compensation for unjust taxation. For a "donut hole," I would pay any tariff. This age excels in sweetmeats. Those produced at Dominic's Bakery, near the police station, are the class of Sleepy Hollow, particularly the pumpkin-flavored variety, which I understand to be seasonal. I shall mourn their absence when the season has passed.

———

While Lieutenant Mills was otherwise occupied, I was able to gather a couple of newspaper articles that I suspect may prove useful. In order to trust her—and, perhaps more important, to gain her trust—I must get to know her better, and she is a deeply private woman. Her down-to-earth practicality has also made it difficult for her to accept the clear signs that she too is a Witness as spoken of in the Revelation of Saint John, though surely she will rise to the responsibility when the occasion demands it. I hope she will forgive my intrusion on her privacy.

SH Officer Headed For Quantico

SLEEPY HOLLOW PUBLIC Safety lieutenant Abigail Mills is set to make the move from local to national law enforcement with her acceptance into the FBI's National Center for the Analysis of Violent Crime (NCAVC) training program. This is the FBI branch responsible for the training and deployment of so-called profilers, investigators assigned to compile evidence-based assessments of a case intended to improve evaluation of potential suspects. Lieutenant Mills will first join the FBI Academy in Quantico, Virginia. Her date of departure from SHPS has not been announced.

Lieutenant Mills was unavailable for comment. SHPS's Sheriff Corbin also declined comment except to say, "Lieutenant Mills is a valued member of the Sleepy Hollow Public Safety force and we anticipate she will be equally valued by the FBI. We wish her the best."

...issing Found

Medical Center ... they were treated ... two teenage girls are ... held today and over ... for observation and are ...pected to be released in ...

...relatively good condition" ...d Dr. Alec Hammond

The Sleepy Hollow Police ...partment ... will not be ...ring any details ...

The ... mother Elizabeth M. A... expressed similar senti... saying.

"I'm just so grateful ... Police and to everyone ... town ..."

At this time there is no indication that any of ... events are connected ... raising serious concer... amongst residents of ... town. With no clear a... coming from local law officials many questio... being asked but few a...

the north side of town just Thursday night. The two girls past the hollow estates were taken to the Sleepy

"Right now we're just glad to see them safe"

GIRLS FOUND UNHARMED IN WOODS

Missing three days

ABIGAIL AND JENNIFER Mills, who went missing three days ago in the woods between Route 9 and the Hudson shore, have been found unharmed. The girls said they went into the woods to explore and lost their way on the afternoon of January 20. A coordinated search involving New York State Police, Westchester County Public Safety officers, and more than one hundred volunteers located the girls not far from a dirt road commonly used by utility workers to maintain power lines in the area.

Garrett Gillespie, 52, who found the girls, was visibly shaken by the ordeal. "I can't stop thinking about all the awful things that could have happened to them," he said. "Little girls like that, all alone. Thank God we found them before . . . well, before something happened."

Abigail and Jennifer were taken to Westchester Memorial Hospital for observation, though neither appeared injured.

other first
ssing after
urn home
:day night
mething was
nner started
aid the girls'
both Mills.
was making
d they would
r that".

ave not had a
nning away.
e honor roll
leepy Hollow
d also partici-
array of extra
vi ies.
n very sweet,
ht, and active
They have no
an away I'm
worried

It's hard
a tree, or
window
Even n
support

priority.
un-turned. W
safely to their mothers. I have de
my department to ensuring their safe return" "This sort of
thing just doesn't happen around here. It's all very unusual but
I and my department are still very confident that we are going
to have a successful and happy res out ion to this case.

										9. Race of Father	
r Father	11. Birthplace (Island, State or Foreign Country)	12a. Usual Occupation								Caucasian	
24										12b. Kind of Business or Industry	0.00
3. Full Maiden Name of Mothe						R				Religious	0.00
5. Age of Mother	16. Birthplace (Island, State or Foreign Country)	17a. Type of Occupation Outside Home During Pregnancy						14. Race of Mother			
22							School Teacher	Caucasian			
certify that the above stated / formation is true and correct / the best of my knowledge.	18a. Signature of Parent or Other Informant							17b. Date Last Worked 10 Apr 63			
hereby certify that this child s born alive on the date and ur stated above.	19a. Signature of Attendant							Parent ☒ 18b. Date of Signature Other ☐ 6 Sept 63			
Date Accepted by Local Reg. 6 Sept 63	21. Signature of Loc						CAPT, MC, USA	M.D. ☒ 19b. Date of Signature D.O. ☐ Midwife ☐ 6 Sept 63 Other ☐			
Evidence for Delayed Filing or Alteration							LT COL, MSC, USA	22. Date Accepted by Reg. General SEP 10 1963			

Yet more supernatural marvels, and again they are tied most intimately to the lives of those around me. Abigail brought me to the scene of a suicide at which the victim's eyes poured sand after her death.

The dead woman was a doctor of the sort known as a psychiatrist, who treated disorders of the mind. One of the signature achievements of this age is proliferating knowledge, and one of its signature obsessions is the creation of specialties. There are doctors for every part of the body, doctors who work only on remedies for single diseases. This Dr. Vega treated the patients at a nearby asylum where, Abigail confided in me, her sister Jennifer has been held for some years. Immediately before the doctor's self-slaughter, as Hamlet would put it, Abigail had a dream in which the doctor, her Captain Irving, and I myself were questioning her about the supernatural vision she and her sister experienced as young girls. Abigail confessed to me that she did not support her sister's truthful narrative, an act of cowardice that has haunted her ever since.

All of these things are related. And so too it emerged was the doctor's suicide, and later the suicide by firearm of the man who found Abigail and Jennifer in the woods. Both were plagued by visions of a demonic creature. Dreams and waking visions are all too often connected; they permit the same portals of entry into the mind and soul. Considering this, we returned to the archives to investigate whether Sheriff Corbin had encountered any demonic entity using dreams. The sand in the doctor's eyes was a physical totem of such magic, as is well-known (or so I'm told—I had never heard of the tale until Abigail recounted it for my benefit) from the old children's tale of the Sandman. In the archive Abigail noticed a symbol and I immediately recognized its meaning: It was a sigil representing the dreaded Mohawk demon Ro'kenhrontyes, which appeared to its victims while they slept.

I spent much time with the Mohawks during the early part of the war. They had no love for the British and were stalwart aides to the colonial forces due to their intimate knowledge of the terrain and prowess on the battlefield. Two Mohawks in particular I counted friends, Wistaron and Wiroh, and it was they who first told me of Ro'kenhrontyes, who killed Wiroh's father for failing a friend in time of need. Supernatural countermeasures, certain symbols, would ward away the demon, also known as the Sandman, if the user of those symbols believed in them. This is something few people understand. The charms and wards known to witches and shamans the world over will not work in the absence of belief. Faith is what gives them power, just as with the sign of the cross.

Other Mohawk creatures whose stories might be of use to us at this or some later time:

Kanontsistóntie's: A disembodied head, with tangled hair, often created by an act of cannibalism (similar origin to the Wendigo of some western tribes) or gruesome murder. It pursues the innocent.

Yakonenyoya'ks: A race of dwarves, often invisible, who occasionally reveal their presence by the sound of their drums. Also known as the Stone Throwers. Mischievous and occasionally a genuine danger, but can be placated by offerings of tobacco or liquor.

Atenenyarhu: A giant, also known as Stone Coat for the hardness of its skin. Like Kanontsistóntie's, sometimes created by an act of cannibalism. Other versions of their tales hold them to be an ancient race created by Flint, the twin brother of Sky Holder, or Maple Sapling. The great leader Hiawatha is said to be a reincarnation of this giant.

Onyare: Horned water creature, akin to the European and Chinese dragon? Said to capsize canoes and devour those within. Hated and opposed by the thunder god Hinun.

Nia'gwahe: Naked Bear, a giant bearlike creature whose fur fell out due to its predilection for human flesh. Can only be killed by attacking the soles of its feet.

We located a Mohawk shaman, but not in the way I would have expected. Abigail informs me that there are three hundred million people living in the United States of America, a number I can scarcely credit. Fewer than three million lived in the colonies at the time of the war's outbreak in 1776. Naturally this hundredfold increase has overspread much of the country's wilderness, where the native tribes made their homes and built their villages. The devastation of the Indian, I understand, is a sordid chapter in the history of the United States. It saddens me to think we repaid the Indians' invaluable cooperation with a century and more of betrayal and war . . . but such is the history. And while history can sometimes be shaped by those who write it, available accounts of European treatment of the Indians are scathing, and therefore believable given the effort that must have been expended to suppress or discredit them. Those few Indians remaining are in large part cordoned off in "reservations," but some live alongside the other races in the gigantic cities and smaller towns of these United States. One such was a man named Seamus (a Mohawk with the name of an Irish hero!), who sold automobiles (cars, as they are colloquially known) from a roadside lot. Abigail knew him, and made introductions. I spoke to him in his native tongue, shocking him, and asked for his assistance with Ro'kenhrontyes. He refused. I had anticipated this, and played my final card, remembering the circumstance that had led to the miserable death of Wiroh's father. If Seamus did not help us, he put himself at the mercy of the demon.

Knowing this danger, Seamus assented. He brought us to a ritual hut and outlined for us what we must do. Defeating Ro'kenhrontyes was only possible by entering his realm and facing the challenge he placed before us. To achieve the penetration of his realm, known to the Mohawk as the Valley of Death, one must be put in a state of waking dream through ritual means. Seamus's version of this ritual incorporated blue jasmine tea and scorpions. I confess to some discomfort at the specter of the scorpion's sting, which I had never experienced but understood to be quite painful. However, the intensity of its sting was matched by the clarity of the vision it provided in conjunction with the tea, which he had altered with other shamanic ingredients unknown to me.

Ro'kenhrontyes kills by forcing his victims to confront endlessly the errors they made that caused pain to their fellow creatures. His Valley of Death is the passage all souls must take from this world to the afterlife, whether it be with the angels or with the infernal hordes. He may not touch those committed to one path or the other; it is those whose fates still hang in the balance who become his prey. When Abigail and I awoke in the Valley of Death, we were separated. Ro'kenhrontyes challenged her by forcing her to face what she had done by lying about her experience seeing the demon. I tried to intervene but was unable to thwart the Sandman until Abigail, displaying a reservoir of courage I suspected must be present in her as it is in her sister, at last admitted her sin and the damage it had caused her sister. In an instant Ro'kenhrontyes froze in a crystalline form and Abigail smashed him to fragments. In doing so, she also saved my life, for the demon's strength had overmastered mine, and I was drowning in sand. Is drowning correct? Suffocating, perhaps. I have never been an habitué of beaches and after this experience am even less inclined to become one.

We emerged from the Valley of Death. The forces of evil, if I may be permitted so melodramatic a phrase, are gathering to oppose the work of the Two Witnesses: Abigail Mills and me. The Hessian, Serilda, now the Sandman of the Mohawk . . . what monstrosity shall we confront next?

Today's events have reminded me of a man called Louis Atay-ataronghta. He and I fought together at the Battle of Oriskany, the most bloody of all the fighting I saw during the course of the war for the future of the American colonies. At this time the Six Nations of the Iroquois were wavering between loyalty to the Crown and allegiance to the colonies. After Oriskany, they would fall into a civil war; before Oriskany, the Oneida were on the colonists' side, the Mohawk divided, and the other tribes tending toward the British side. At Oriskany many Mohawks fought with the British, who ambushed a relief column making for Fort Stanwix. It was a terrible slaughter. Louis, one of the few Mohawks who fought for the colonial forces that day, saved my life.

Given the elaborate operation involved in firing a musket in 1776, even the fastest of men could not reload in less than fifteen seconds, and most could only accomplish it in twenty or more. During that pause, when a soldier was occupied with the business of tearing open cartridges of powder and so forth, he was vulnerable to attack. The Indians fighting with the British soon learned that once a soldier fired, if he could be engaged at arm's length before reloading his musket, he was no match for a skilled wielder of a tomahawk or spear. A great many of the colonists met their end in this way during the engagement at Oriskany—I would have joined them had it not been for the quick reflexes of Louis, who saw a Mohawk moving to take me as I fumbled whilst reloading.

I was at Oriskany with the relief column because General Washington had sent me. Why, I did not know at the time—although now, with the advantage of hindsight and the revelations contained in his Bible, I suspect something supernatural was afoot. All I knew then was that I was accompanying a column sent in relief to the commander of the besieged fort, Colonel Peter Gansevoort.

Needing to catch up with the caravan, which had left some days before, I sought Louis's knowledge of the terrain to make up time and join the resupply effort before it arrived. As events transpired, we had just made contact with the relief effort's commander, Nicholas Herkimer, when the British and their Iroquois allies attacked. The ambush resulted in the loss of the artifact to the British—but only temporarily, as shortly thereafter I and a small group of rebels sallied out from the fort under cover of darkness and sacked the British encampment. We burned their supplies and escaped, recovering the artifact, which Colonel Gansevoort then carried to Fort Saratoga when the siege was lifted.

I saw a great many men die during those days. For miles around, one could stumble across the bodies of those fallen in the battle, as skirmishes spread through the entirety of the valley. My lasting impression of Oriskany, however, is the lightning quickness of Louis Atayataronghta, striking seemingly out of nowhere to bury his tomahawk in the head of a fellow Mohawk who was about to strike me down. I know not what became of him after the war.

———

Two other developments of note:

One is that Captain Irving continues to walk his narrow path between permitting us to work and keeping the knowledge of our work from those who would not be so sympathetic. He suggested—in a tone that I took to mean a polite command—that we commence using the archives as our base of operations, to keep us out of sight of the rest of the constabulary and those who monitor them. We agreed, happily on my part.

Second: I spoke with Abigail's sister, Jennifer, who agreed to see me despite her refusal of a visit from her own sister. There is genuine steel in that young woman, forged and tempered by her experience. From the files kept by Sheriff Corbin I was able to extract a less-than-diligent assessment of her condition, conducted on the occasion of one of her multiple confinements in a mental institution. Apparently she was freed on several occasions for a short period of time, and incarcerated again each time, the last for the theft of survival equipment. She believes in the approach of the End of Days and did not flinch when I broached the topic, or when I revealed to her that the Horsemen were soon to ride. She is angry and suspicious, rightfully so—but when I asked her for aid in our struggle, she did not refuse. I write this now because after our battle with Ro'kenhrontyes, Abigail rode her newfound wave of courage to the asylum in Tarrytown, and found that Jennifer had escaped.

[October 9]

We were given twelve hours to find Jennifer before Captain Irving began a manhunt. This courtesy, scant as it was, proved enough. As it happened, we needed much less, as a visit to the Mills sisters' last foster mother revealed the location of Jennifer's sanctuary, a place whence she fled at those moments when her troubles grew too great—or, as Abigail and I learned, when she became entangled in events which might endanger her foster family or other innocents. When we arrived at the specified location, a cabin near a charming small body of water known by the equally charming name of Trout Lake, Abigail and I learned quite a lot in little time.

First, the cabin had belonged to Sheriff Corbin. Photographic evidence indicated that the sheriff and Jennifer were acquainted. This news was a considerable shock to Abigail, perhaps even more than what transpired immediately thereafter.

Second, Lieutenant Mills possesses certain skills ordinarily the province of her criminal counterparts. She dismantled the cabin's lock with an alacrity I could only admire, hearkening back no doubt to her own days as a lawless youth.

Third, Jennifer was there ahead of us, and armed. She and her sister stood like duelists awaiting the command to fire while I endeavored to restore calm. This was successful, and instead of firing on one another, the two sisters began to exchange information. Jennifer recounted Corbin's belief in her version of the sisters' childhood experience. He sent her on a number of secret errands to different parts of the world, for the purpose of collecting rare artifacts that would contribute to his research. This accounted for the records of her travels Abigail discovered when we began our search.

Jennifer's story grew yet stranger, as she recounted a visit from Corbin the night before his murder—and, therefore, the night before I awoke in the cave. He came to her and warned her of his death, drawing a pledge from her that she would protect a sextant hidden in the cabin. She produced it for us, and I was hardly able to believe what I saw, for the sextant was scored with marks I had seen before.

Every American knows of the Boston Tea Party, but at the same time every American knows nothing about it—beginning with the name, which is quite glib in light of what transpired on the Boston wharves that night. We called it "the destruction of the tea" at the time, and understood our actions to be very serious. The purported goal, to protest ruinous taxes imposed by King George III, was certainly valid; yet the specific choices made by

Readmitted

[Confidential]

PATIENT INTAKE ASSESSMENT

Jennifer Mills presents as a lucid, somewhat aggressive African-American female of seventeen. She stands five feet five inches tall and is extremely physically fit. She is aware of her involuntary commitment (her third) and understands she has been committed due to acts of vandalism and threatened violence, as well as repeated references to such topics as the end of the world. These suggest a paranoid or paranoid schizophrenic disorder. Testing will continue along those lines. This impression is further strengthened by Jennifer's desire to train in martial arts and acquire weapons. She states that a war is coming and she will be required to fight. Apocalyptic visions of this sort are atypical in Jennifer's demographic and are considered another marker of the severity of her mental illness.

Jennifer's history includes a number of arrests and citations for breaking and entering, theft, and possession of stolen goods. She has avoided incarceration in state juvenile facilities due to her psychiatric issues stemming from an as yet undisclosed childhood trauma, which occurred during a three-day period in January 2001 when she and her sister, Abigail (now in foster care), were lost in the woods at the edge of Sleepy Hollow's boundaries. Jennifer alleges that the two girls encountered a supernatural being. Abigail denies this. There exists palpable tension between the two sisters, at least in Jennifer's view. ▮▮▮

The natural interpretation of Jennifer's paranoid tenden-
cies and her mythologizing of her childhood trauma is that
she has suffered some manner of sexual abuse. Jennifer
denies this and is vehement about the particulars of her
story. ███
███
███████████████████ Therapy and antianxiety medication are
indicated; a physician consult will be scheduled with Dr.
Vega, who conducted Jennifer's courses of therapy during
Jennifer's previous commitments to TPH.

Signed,

Lucinda Echevarria

Lucinda Echevarria, RN
March 21, 2008

the Sons of Liberty, perpetrators of this famous dissent, masked a more devious goal. I know this because I was there. I saw the costumed revelers dumping tea in the harbor, and I saw the Red-coats responding. While they were so engaged, I and my commander, a Virginia militiaman by the name of Doxford, led an armed party to seize the true object of the mission. We were sent by General Washington himself, who commanded us to capture a weapon of unknown nature held by the British on a pier at Boston Harbor on Griffin's Wharf. The ships moored there made for a convenient diversion, nothing more; had they held rum or coffee or beaver pelts, our men in Mohawk costume would have thrown those into the harbor with gusto equal to that they demonstrated with the casks of tea. The tea ships were there, and the question of taxes and tea was a stormy one. Thus the way was paved for our mission.

We crept to the storehouse on the wharf and Doxford commanded me to stand watch outside. A moment later a tremendous explosion sounded and much of the storehouse was destroyed. I ran to the aid of my comrades and found everyone inside dead, including a Hessian terribly mangled by the grenade he had set off to defend the object we had come to collect. The fire and collapsed ruins made my task exceedingly difficult, but near the Hessian's body I found a small chest made of stone. Without opening it or making any effort to ascertain its contents, I conveyed it to General Washington, along with a ciphered report detailing the night's events. Then, in the next years, I thought no more of it; such tasks were quite common in the years leading up to the rebellion, and indeed throughout the years of active conflict. Looking back on it, I think that of all the tasks General Washington set me, this was hardly the most unusual.

I recounted this tale for Abigail and Miss Jenny while I examined the sextant, and after a moment I guessed its function. With a beam powered by batteries—a flashlight, so called, and here again I must note the incomprehensible advance of batteries over the initial investigations of Messrs. Franklin and Leyden—I projected an image via the sextant and instantly identified it as a map of Sleepy Hollow. From my time, at that. A location marked on this map, I felt certain, would hold the chest whose remembered markings had allowed me to recognize the nature of the sextant. I am coming to believe I have awakened into a world where no coincidence exists, or is possible.

Gunfire interrupted us then, and three bandits assaulted the cabin. I have been in a number of battles, but no volley of musketry or artillery had prepared me for the bludgeoning barrage of these modern weapons. We returned their fire, however, and though two of the miscreants escaped with the sextant, we held the third captive, who bore a tattoo identifying him as a Hessian. I interrogated him in German, and with the fearlessness and arrogance common to his cohort, he revealed without hesitation that the box contained the Lesser Key of Solomon. He had no fear of revealing this, he said, because Sleepy Hollow was rife with Hessians, hiding as it were in plain sight.

Abigail communicated with Captain Irving, and he led a search to this man Gunther's house. There they discovered all manner of esoterica and occult paraphernalia. Abigail demanded of Gunther that he reveal the name of the Hessians' leader and he replied that they had already seen him. The blurred demonic figure—of the Mills girls' childhood terror, of Katrina's otherworldly prison—was none other than the demon Moloch himself. It was he who had summoned the Horsemen, he who returned evil spirits to the world. We pressed Gunther further, but with a final salute to his demonic allegiance—*Moloch erheben*—he committed suicide by means of a pill hidden in his mouth.

Moloch erheben. "Moloch rises."

MOLOCH. Attested by the ancients as a god requiring the sacrifice of children by fire. Later understood as a demon, whose favor could only be gained through terrible sacrifice. Records from Carthage suggest the sacrifice of hundreds of children at once—

I cannot bear to write of this anymore. The barbarity of mankind overwhelms me at times, when I am tired and sleeping poorly. All cultures create demons to explain their worst qualities, but we need no demons to excuse our pillage and rapine; it is in us. I have witnessed it today and it is, I fear, my destiny to witness a great deal more. Nevertheless, demons are real. Perhaps they are created from the very stuff of our transgressions, or perhaps they have always been, and alter their appearance to suit the stories we tell of them. Who may know? The Moloch of the ancients would watch my suffering and approve, though it would not satisfy him. Wherever his name appears, there is soon to come accounts of the worst of human behavior.

He is our enemy now, it seems—a warrior against heaven. He is real, and pitiless, and will destroy all those who refuse their consent to be his thralls. The purest distillation of Moloch's character comes from the pages of Milton. I first read *Paradise Lost* before I came to Oxford, when I was still a boy, but no force of nature or man could tear these lines from my mind. I seem to hear Moloch's voice as if the council of his fellow fallen angels was taking place within my brain.

> ...(I)f there be in Hell
> Fear to be worse destroy'd: what can be worse
> Then to dwell here, driv'n out from bliss, condemn'd
> In this abhorred deep to utter woe;
> Where pain of unextinguishable fire
> Must exercise us without hope of end
> The Vassals of his anger, when the Scourge
> Inexorably, and the torturing houre
> Calls us to Penance? More destroy'd then thus
> We should be quite abolisht and expire.
> What fear we then? what doubt we to incense
> His utmost ire? which to the highth enrag'd,
> Will either quite consume us, and reduce
> To nothing this essential, happier farr
> Then miserable to have eternal being:
> Or if our substance be indeed Divine,
> And cannot cease to be, we are at worst
> On this side nothing; and by proof we feel
> Our power sufficient to disturb his Heav'n,
> And with perpetual inrodes to Allarme,
> Though inaccessible, his fatal Throne:
> Which if not Victory is yet Revenge.

That quieted my mind. The pen does the will of the brain, the hand is the instrument. Yet the sentiments expressed are anything but tranquil. If this Moloch of the Hessians is the same warlike spirit Milton knew (for one who has seen what I have seen must surely believe that Milton knew rather than invented; a visionary he was despite his blindness, or indeed perhaps because of it)—if this Moloch is the same, we are in for a weary struggle, and only faith will permit us to believe in our eventual triumph.

MOLOCH

An 18th-century German illustration of Moloch ("Der Götze Moloch" i.e. The Idol Moloch).

"FIRST MOLOCH, HORRID KING
BESMEAR'D WITH BLOOD
OF HUMAN SACRIFICE, AND PARENTS
TEARS,
THOUGH, FOR THE NOYSE OF DRUMS
AND TIMBRELS LOUD,
THEIR CHILDREN'S CRIES UNHEARD THAT
PASSED THROUGH FIRE
TO HIS GRIM IDOL. HIM THE
AMMONITE
WORSHIPT IN RABBA AND HER WATRY
PLAIN,
IN ARGOB AND IN BASAN, TO THE
STREAM
OF UTMOST ARNON. NOR CONTENT
WITH SUCH
AUDACIOUS NEIGHBOURHOOD, THE
WISEST HEART

William Blake (1809, The Flight of Moloch, watercolour, 25.7 x 19.7 cm. One of Blake's illustrations of On the Morning of Christ's Nativity, the poem by John Milton

DEMONIC SYMBOLS

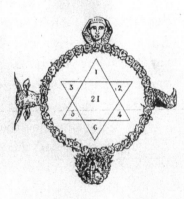

President Foras

Duke Berith

Duke Astaroth

Marquis Forneus

President Foras

King Amadeus

Prince & President Gaap

Count Furfur

Marquis Marchosias

Prince Stolas

I have read of the Lesser Key of Solomon in any number of texts on demonology. First known during the Crusades, it came under the protection of the Knights Templar until its location was lost following their denunciation and bloody suppression by Philip IV of France and Pope Clement V. It is a book whose contents teach the would-be sorcerer the means of unlocking a door to the seventh circle of hell, where seventy-two demons wait eternally for their opportunity to escape into our world. By its other name, the Lemegeton, it has existed since medieval times, and was compiled from yet older sources.

I have seen copies of this book before, yet it appeared quite differently to the Hessians this day. One suspects that is due to Moloch's power and control. Miss Jenny seems to know of the book as well, and she also has knowledge of the lore of the Knights Templar, which I would not have expected in a woman of her tender years. She and Abigail both seem to me, in the phrase of Juliet's father, but strangers to this world as yet . . . although if one were to count up our birthdays, mine would not number too differently from theirs. I must remember this, lest I appear patronizing to two such vigorously intelligent and competent young women.

Not for the first time—nor, I hope, for the last—my gift of memory played its part, as I was able to sketch out the map as I had seen it projected from the sextant. Abigail noted the marked location, where General Washington had the chest containing the Lemegeton buried, as currently occupied by the Dutch Reformed Church—reformed from what, I had occasion to wonder—and we made haste to get there before the two other Hessians could make the same discovery and unlock the awful potential inherent in the Lesser Key.

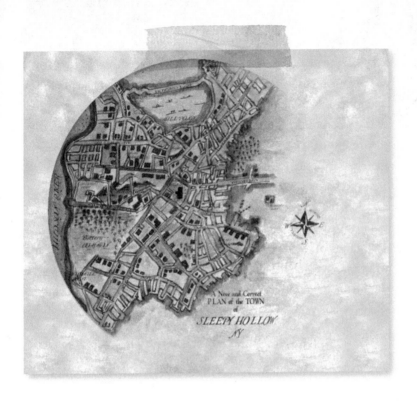

A New and Correct
PLAN of the TOWN
of
SLEEPY HOLLOW
NY

Miss Jenny's courage under fire was quite impressive to me, and I expressed this to her, whereupon she explained that during the course of her travels in Sheriff Corbin's service, she had seen combat with rebellious forces in Mexico and what she called South Sudan. I know of the Sudan only as the region in Africa where the Blue and White Nile flow together, and that thanks only to the accounts of explorers read in the British Library during my early studies. So too with a nation now called Somalia, which I understand to be in the Horn of Africa, near the ancient civilization of Ethiopia—where, it is said, the Ark of the Covenant itself is hidden away and guarded by the deathless resolve of the Knights Templar and their descendants.

There was no time to speak in more depth, for we had arrived at the Dutch Reformed Church. We engaged the two Hessians as they were sacrilegiously performing the Lesser Key's ritual of opening in the sanctuary. Within a burning pentagram composed of the pages of the book itself, the seventy-two demons strained at the thinning membrane separating them from our world and their infernal plane. Jennifer again demonstrated her bravery, as with a gun to her head she encouraged Abigail to think of stopping the ritual instead of protecting her. Abigail refused either choice, finding instead the third way of throwing the book itself into the fire. The agony of the demons as they were driven back from our world was terrible to hear, and driven by the fury of battle, I drove one of the Hessians into the closing portal, consigning him to the hell he wished to serve.

———————————

A recollection of a humorous nature: NorthStar. Some cars are equipped with a means of communicating with distant monitors who address the driver in the event of a mishap. The technology involved is difficult to explain, it seems. I gather it has something to do with machines orbiting Earth itself, miniature mechanical moons numbering in the thousands, each of which receives and transmits signals by means of some electrical field or beam. The telephones in every pocket operate using the same mechanism. How the electrical field transmits sound is a mystery to me.

In any event, Abigail's car emitted some sort of signal, to which one of these NorthStar monitors, a young lady named Yolanda, responded. I spoke to her and assured her nothing was amiss, after which we struck up a heartfelt conversation. This young woman was lovelorn and uncertain how to answer the edicts of the heart, and she confided in me. It being churlish to do otherwise, I answered her confidences with such advice as I deemed appropriate. How incongruous in the midst of a war between heaven and hell, to find oneself playing soothsayer to an utter stranger—and, what is more, an utter stranger who might have been on the very moon. I could not have anticipated that a disembodied voice speaking to me through the car would require counsel, but such is what I endeavored to provide. And indeed she too salved some of my emotional wounds; I spoke to her of Katrina, my love for her, and the difficulties of our separation. Yolanda was a lovely young woman, and a comfort in a lonely time.

Also of interest today: Captain Irving suspects a Hessian turncoat in the ranks of his constabulary. Spy hunters of some sort are coming from Manhattan, which from what I understand is now one of the world's great cities, with a population of some sixteen million. I remember traveling there on errands for General Washington, when it was a settlement at the island's tip, thickly forested and well watered by not just the Hudson and Haarlem Rivers but numerous smaller streams as well. It was much smaller than Boston or Philadelphia then, but in the two centuries since it has far outstripped them.

I remember New York as a thriving port, where the Dutch presence was still visible not only in the names of streets and landmarks but in the practical and thrifty ways of its citizens. Not for them the pretensions of Boston or the lofty ruminations of the Philadelphian; New York was a city where there was much to do, and the people there set about doing it. I understand it is now much the same, and has acquired a reputation for brusqueness as well. It was one of my favorites of all American settlements; I do hope to see what has become of it.

Another product of my researches, this bit of doggerel, apparently known as the "Boston Toast":

> *And this is good old Boston,*
> *The home of the bean and the cod.*
> *Where the Lowells talk only to Cabots,*
> *And the Cabots talk only to God.*

Ha! Quite so. Even when I knew that city, its social snobbery was renowned.

I have not dreamed of Katrina in several days. Optimism is my true nature, but even so I fear the worst.

[October 14]

Walking down the street today, innocently preoccupied with the eternal war of good against evil (as one in my position often is), I collided with a woman running around the corner of the building from which I had just then emerged. She showered me with invective, and I made my excuses, although I am certain the fault was hers. Then she ran on after resetting her wristwatch. Consulting Abigail, I learned I had encountered a "jogger." These, it seems, are people who run long distances for the sake of nothing more than running. I hereby deem this a psychological disability, and I said as much to Abigail.

Her response? A phrase I believe I shall adopt: "Don't knock it 'til you try it."

Abigail has gained conservatorship over her sister, a step toward securing Jennifer's freedom from the apparatus of the state. In other salutary news, I am free of the sterile environs of the motel room and am now quartered in Corbin's cabin. It suits me. There is less plastic here. More of this when I have set down the day's events, which include a brush with death not by demonic means but by a more prosaic road to mortality: a disease of unknown origin.

It began with a lost boy, sick and speaking a language no one could understand. Abigail and I responded, as did medical personnel, and I realized he was speaking Middle English. The vowel sounds and lack of Latinate constructions make this period of the English language quite distinct from both its Anglo-Saxon ancestor and modern English descendant. I followed him to the hospital and continued questioning him. He gave his name as Thomas Grey and said his home was Roanoke. At this point our conversation was truncated by the officials in charge of halting the spread of the boy's disease, which had already infected the medic who first attempted to treat him. Abigail and I were fortunate to escape quarantine ourselves.

From the boy's dress, demeanor, and antiquated language, I surmised he spoke not of the present-day Roanoke, Virginia, but the lost colony of Roanoke, one of the first great mysteries of the European settlement of this continent. A thriving community founded in the sixteenth century, it vanished during the period of a single year, without any known cause. The story of Roanoke had already entered the colonial mythology when I first crossed the Atlantic in 1770, and as Abigail and I began our researches we found that the myths and legends had proliferated since then. How odd that here in the twenty-first century, I still find occasion to make use of my hard-won fluency in the Middle English of the fifteenth!

We returned to the place where the boy was first spotted,

and I retraced his steps, putting to good use tracking skills I had learned as a youth foxhunting, and which were honed to excellency (I acknowledge the immodesty, but 'tis true) by scouting missions in the company of Mohawks. There were two sets of tracks, which lent credence to young Thomas's story of an *euel þerne*—an evil girl—and this story grew yet more credible when the second set of tracks simply vanished. Thomas's own tracks grew confused at that point, and rushed. I saw the ragged panic in his stride. A skilled tracker can tell much about a person's emotions and behaviors by the minutiae of that person's footprints: where the weight falls hardest, whether the spacing between prints is even, a dozen or a hundred different factors. It was clear Thomas was lost once this second set of prints disappeared, and it was not difficult to infer the cause. A demon had misled the boy.

By means of a hidden bridge (and avoiding an amphibious guardian creature which I am glad to report I know of only at a distance) Abigail and I found our way across the bog to the island, and there a wonder awaited us. Roanoke, it seemed, had survived, an idyllic village arranged around a well, with people looking happy and content—their visible black veins notwithstanding. They all had the plague that was proving so lethal in the world outside, yet none of them appeared the least affected by it. I spoke to the prefect of the colony—he too spoke in a version of the language that seemed antiquated even for 1590, which he cited as the year of their exodus from Virginia. The plague began to spread among them in that year, and they understood that they were to leave Roanoke, trusting in their Creator to find a new home. The colony's most famous resident, the first English child born in North America, little Virginia Dare, died of the plague. Her spirit inhabited a white doe, the prefect recounted, and the guidance of that doe led the colony to their new home. As long as they remained on their hidden island, protected by the doe, the progress of the disease was arrested.

Thomas Grey, upon leaving the island, suffered the progression of the disease anew. The prefect believed him misguided by the devil; I for my part suspected Moloch.

I asked him what was to be done. He had a simple answer: Return Thomas Grey to the island so that he could be healed and the worsening of his disease prevented. This seemed simple enough, but as with all matters related to the evils lurking in and around Sleepy Hollow, first impressions were thoroughly deceptive. The moment I exited the secret island and returned to the hospital—conferring with Abigail along the way regarding the best method by which we might free young Thomas and return him to his magically sequestered people—I too began to manifest the dread symptoms of the black-vein plague.

Quite a number of things transpired during the past few hours, few of which I can recount firsthand, for the reason that I was under involuntary sedation. I can offer direct testimony of the welcome return—despite the trying circumstances—of my wife in a dream. She evinced concern upon seeing me, knowing that my presence in her Mirror World while I was not asleep could only mean I hovered near death. I learned to my dismay that the forested prison was in fact Purgatory, where souls persist until the heavenly authorities decree they have expiated their earthly transgressions. What could she have done to be consigned to such a place? Was her witchcraft the cause—or was her imprisonment there a result of Moloch's machinations? I asked her and she demurred; I pressed her and she might have offered a hint—or might not—but at that moment Moloch struck. My Purgatory self was more vigorous than my sedated physical self, to be sure, and I was able to escape, swearing I would return. I know not by what means I was able to traverse the distance between near-death and full wakefulness again—save through the willpower all humans possess but so few ever employ fully—but I awoke in the hospital again and quickly conveyed to Abigail my recent discoveries. The disease officials tried to prevent our exit, but Captain Irving again proved that whatever his reservations, his heart is, as they say, in the right place.

I made it to the island with the very last of my strength and the most crucial under the looming threat of the Horseman of Pestilence—for it was he who had infected the Roanoke colonists and he who would burst through into our world if the black-vein plague spread to enough citizens. The second Horseman, so soon! How quickly might we get our first inklings of the third? The fourth? We fought back, staying ahead of the Horseman of Pestilence long enough to submerge my failing body in the artesian water of the well at the center of the island. The same cure was attempted simultaneously for Thomas Grey, but he did not survive . . . and in a revelation, it became apparent that he had not been alive for quite some time. His spirit rose away, and then the spirits of the other island colonists joined his. The Horseman of Pestilence, thwarted, returned whence he had come, and the darkest times of tribulation were delayed . . . for how long, it is not given us to know.

When the souls had passed on, I realized I had moved from one Purgatory to another of sorts, where the souls of the Roanoke colonists had been held these five centuries. Abigail and I, as Witnesses, had released them—and we had also forestalled the appearance of the Horseman of Pestilence. All in all, as it is commonly said in this age, a pretty good day's work.

It was a moment of awe, to understand what the burden and power of a Witness truly was. Then we stood, Abigail and I, in a long-overgrown ruin, the only discernible sign of its ever having been inhabited the remains of the artesian well. I was saddened by its passing; I felt as if I belonged there, or at the very least that this hidden island, ensorcelled though it may have been, brought into stark relief that degree to which I was alone in Abigail's time. This age of plastic and satellites, cars and endless cities, where everything smells like the river downstream from a tannery . . . it is not mine. It will never be mine.

Yet it is the age in which I now live—the age in which I continue to serve the cause I first joined in the long-withered year of 1771. Abigail was a great help to me in this moment. We have a connection, not just due to our mutual task as Witnesses; something more personal, transcending the gulfs and barriers of age, or race, of history. . . .

I believe there is a genuine trust between us now. I have certainly entrusted her with my life, and she has reciprocated. We were thrown together by dire circumstance, and might have allowed mutual suspicion to weaken us in the face of deadly threats; but happily we have made a better choice. I am glad to count her as an ally, and perhaps a friend as well.

Having viewed a modern hospital, it occurs to me now that this age is a fine one in which to be sick or injured. No one dies of gangrene or battlefield infection thanks to drugs known as antibiotics (one apparently created during an experiment on the growth of mold!). Amputations by bone saw, sterilized by whiskey, and suffered by means of biting down on a stick—these are unknown. Injections forestall the spread of diseases that ravaged my age: Smallpox has been eradicated! Scarlet fever, diphtheria, measles . . . these are now so uncommon that their appearance is newsworthy.

What a difference this would have made to the colonial militias. They were sick, and poorly nourished, and fell in droves to scythes of disease. Had we this medical science, the Revolution would have been over before 1781 . . . and perhaps I would never have encountered the Hessian; thus it is demonstrated, perhaps, that things occur in the manner they are destined to occur.

———

Now I am back in the cabin. Still I am thinking of Roanoke, and the world before engines and telephones and videotape and NorthStar and flashlights—before, to be brief, this age wherein everything seems always to happen at once. I learned how to use one of these iPhones (what arrant foolishness, this transposition of the initial capital to the interior of a word). Perhaps I am slowly assimilating this age, or it is assimilating me. . . .

It is time to sleep, but I cannot stop thinking of the way Moloch misled the boy Thomas Grey, gave him flesh and drew him out into Sleepy Hollow, seeking to spread his disease. The advent of the Horseman of Pestilence cannot be far away, if it has not happened already.

In honor of young Thomas Grey, I recall the last lines of a poem by his near namesake, which all young men of sentiment memorized when I was a boy. The entire poem invariably brings me to melancholy, and I fear melancholy is too much to face this eve—perhaps another, when Katrina and I might again meet face-to-face. For the touch of her hand on mine, I would consider the Faustian bargain.

From Gray:

The Epitaph

Here rests his head upon the lap of earth
A youth to fortune and to fame unknown.
Fair Science frowned not on his humble birth,
And Melancholy marked him for her own.

Large was his bounty, and his soul sincere,
Heaven did a recompense as largely send:
He gave to Misery all he had, a tear,
He gained from Heaven ('twas all he wished) a friend.

No farther seek his merits to disclose,
Or draw his frailties from their dread abode,
(There they alike in trembling hope repose)
The bosom of his Father and his God.

[October 15]

I have learned a timely and welcome lesson yesterday and today:
The past is ever present. The Sleepy Hollow I knew in 1781 is still
here, hidden perhaps from those who know not how to look for
it, but here nonetheless. Recent events have put me again in the
company of men who see this past, men who exist in a mysterious
network of whispers and secrets. I am speaking of the Freemasons, a most secretive brotherhood who know all too well the cost
when good men fail to heed the dictates of their consciences. I was
reminded of them a week or so hence when I overheard a conversation about capital punishment, and was struck by its rarity and
by the vehemence of the opposition to the practice. The people of
this age have little idea how dramatically the estimation of human
life has been altered by the emergence of republican government.
I can say this having been born in an age when young boys were

still routinely hanged for stealing food, and less than a century removed from Britain's last execution by drawing and quartering. In the colonies, shortly after my arrival, I witnessed not just acts of extreme brutality but a routine snuffing out of lives like so many candles before bed—the offhand execution of human beings innocent of any crime save for their desire to be free of oppression. It was on one such occasion that Colonel Tarleton, doubtless without intending to do so, effected that meeting from which the rest of my life has unspooled.

Arthur Bernard was a man of courage, a black man who envisioned the American colonies as a land where his people could breathe free—despite the sordid history of slavery on which the prosperity of the colonies was built—and a writer of lucidity and great influence. He wrote pseudonymously, as so many did then, knowing the British were watching the American pamphleteering presses and suppressing those they found objectionable. I knew of him (more accurately of his nom de plume, Cicero) through his connection to the thinkers arguing their visions of what a free America might be . . . and it was also those connections that made him a target for Tarleton. Bernard suffered at the hands of Tarleton's brutes and only the resolute interference of a young Quaker woman (or so she presented herself) by the name of Katrina saved him further maltreatment. She was a marvelous young woman, courageous and utterly committed to the ideals of her sect (I write this meaning Quakerism, and realizing at the same time how it might be taken to refer to her less pious activities). She caught my eye from the beginning, and I believed I hers; and subsequent events were to prove this impression correct. After she attended to Arthur, I was placed in the untenable position of being forced to prove my loyalty to the Crown by executing him. I refused, and—

Oh. I remember. Or no, that is a foolish thing to write. I always remember. What I mean is that I now understand what I remember; I no longer cover it over with a palimpsest of explanations and rationalizations. For years I tried to convince myself that at the moment of Arthur Bernard's death, I had not really seen the officer Tarleton assume a demonic aspect. For how could I have? There were no demons. In 1771, for me, there were no witches or undead Hessians, no demons or monsters, no adversaries but the flesh-and-blood men on the other side of the firing lines.

Now, having learned the truth—or at least part of it—regarding my reawakening, I know I did in fact see Tarleton's true nature. It was my thinking mind that introduced the error, being unable to accept the reality of what it perceived.

To return to the line of thought that first brought the Freemasons to mind: Arthur Bernard's last words to me were an instruction to find Katrina and speak to her the words *Ordo ab Chao*. This, it emerged, was the pass phrase that gained one access to the Freemasons; I quickly became acquainted with the known history of this august organization—as a network of professional men dedicated to the compass and square, or the advancement of civilized ideals. Now I am curious to learn more of the Freemasons' other activities—for nothing, it seems, is as I believed it to be before. More important, Bernard's request offered me the chance to make my future wife's acquaintance. Her mysteries were a wonder to me then, and they remain so now; she was more than a nurse, more even than a witch whose magical powers served the highest of human ideals.

I believe Tarleton was the first demon I ever saw—though knowing the powers of disguise possessed by the infernal entities, I confess I cannot be certain. At the time I believed I had become aware of a great gift, to penetrate the disguises of demons walking in human form and know them for what they were. Perhaps I still possess it.

Demons masquerade as men, and every face seems to hide a secret. One makes decisions in this atmosphere, and the only choice is to do what is right, and let the consequences be what they will.

That, in short, is how I came to shift my allegiance from Crown to colony.

———————

The Freemasons have something of a reputation in this time as a social club, save for among the conspiracy-minded, who view them as a secret society bent on the clandestine control of the world. I am a Freemason myself, and had until recently believed them to be men of goodwill who used their common connection to further goals they deemed beneficial to all humanity. If their methods demanded secrecy, so be it; and from that embrace of secrecy the wilder notions about the Freemasons have developed. Masons protect each other, and they do what they can to ensure the integrity of the brotherhood (not yet a sisterhood as well, at least not here; the Freemasons almost alone seem to have preserved themselves as a bastion of the masculine, for good or ill). Where the lovers of conspiracy misunderstand the Freemasons is in their idea that all Masons seek power. In fact they are quite rigorous about setting the well-being of humanity above the survival of any individual member—as I knew before and as I learned anew this past day.

The Freemasons are alive and well in Sleepy Hollow, and they learned of my connection with the Hessian. They abducted me, with no more force than was necessary, and argued quite reasonably that since I was linked by blood to the Hessian it was my responsibility to weaken the Hessian by ending my own life. This logic, cold as it seems, was unassailable. In the presence of Abigail, I drank the poison they proffered, knowing that this suicidal act— so contrary to my will and the traditions of my people and my reli-gion—was for the best. What matters one man's death, set against the survival of so many others who would thereby be spared the wrath of the Horsemen and their demonic legions?

I was saved, however, by a Sin Eater, a man named Henry Parish, bearer of a gift that for most of his life felt like a curse. It was he who severed the link between the Hessian and myself, and he who taught me an invaluable lesson. For the Sin Eater cannot simply take sins away; he can only assist in their absolution when the sinner has come to understand the true nature of the sin and atoned for it. My sins—and this is why I thought at such length of Arthur Bernard—included not acting quickly enough to aid good men in peril. Regret for those sins made me vulnerable to the con-nection with the Hessian, for regret on its own is a sin of another kind, a self-indulgence. Only when regret is partnered with for-giveness and resolve to go forth and sin no more, in the words of the Gospels, does it gain any redemptive power. So Henry Parish taught me, and when I understood this my blood separated from the Hessian's. Then Parish could perform his strange inverted communion, sopping up some of the Hessian's blood—bled from my own veins—with bread and eating it. He appeared to me as Arthur Bernard for a moment, taking on the likeness of that reso-lute fighter for independence and teaching me that from regret and guilt must be fashioned a newly strengthened resolve.

That act also purged the poison from my body, saving my life and returning me to fitness for the battle against the Horseman and his allies. I have been on the point of death thrice now in these past several weeks (so it seems to me, though the first time my life was saved was more than two hundred years ago!)—surely greater forces than mortal will are at work. I am a Witness, and I see around me the measures people of good heart will take to further our cause. We shall prevail.

———————

Sin Eaters. The practice is as ancient as the idea of sin, and I am well familiar with it from my studies of the history of the more backward regions of Britain. There the Sin Eater often lived severed from the life of his community, marked out by his dark gift. When death was near—or when a sinner had just passed on from this life—the Sin Eater was given a piece of bread and a bowl of beer. In consuming these, he ritually consumed the sins of the departed and sanctified the fleeing spirit. The success of the ritual was typically announced by a short speech: I once saw it recorded as *I give easement and rest now to thee, dear man. Come not down the lanes or in our meadows. And for thy peace I pawn my own soul. Amen.* Ritual words, which give comfort and ease in the way ritual is supposed to.

The custom survives on these shores as well. I saw the small cakes and loaves prepared at funerals among the Dutch, to be ritually eaten by the relatives of the deceased. (And by *Dutch* here I mean Germans, by the corruption of *Deutsch* to *Dutch* so common in the colonies.) To pawn one's own soul—for whoever asks—this is a courage I cannot imagine possessing. Yet Henry Parish has it, and he is only the latest in a lineage of such brave lonely souls stretching back into the mists of prehistory.

Jennifer Mills, I learned, went in search of a Sin Eater on behalf of Sheriff Corbin. She traveled the world without success, visiting Africa and Japan. I envy this young woman her world travels. I saw Paris as a young man, and have rested my eyes on the finer prospects of Britain—I visited each of the thirteen colonies in the years before they banded together to form the nascent United States—yet set against the immensity of this world and the marvelous variety of its peoples, my travels seem like the first steps of a toddler proud to traverse the arm's length from the kitchen chair to his father's waiting embrace.

What other folkloric constructs await? Am I soon to encounter a wandering scapegoat, laden with the sins of this tribe and cast out into the concrete deserts? I hope to travel in this modern America, and perhaps to see its more mundane wonders as I fight the occult machinations behind the shiny surface. The West! No Englishman had gone farther than the great Mississippi, known as the Father of Waters, in my time. Now there are mighty cities on the Pacific coast, named by the Spaniards who laid their first stones: Los Angeles, San Francisco. The Rocky Mountains! The Grand Canyon! How I would love to see these fabled places.

These are plans for a future time. A time of peace. For now, it must suffice that I am free of the Hessian—and, presumably, he of me. Now either of us may die.

Whilst considering the Hessians and the Freemasons, the Radiant Heart and the Blood Moon—in short, the many secret societies that have proliferated in Sleepy Hollow over the centuries—I had a curious idea. For we have seen as yet no action of a most clandestine club that Benjamin Franklin put me in mind of many years ago, and I might have expected them to be involved in events so portentous as those we have lately experienced. A maddening figure, Franklin. Bombastic and pompous, absentminded and arrogant—yet at the same time undeniably witty, fine company at supper, and a perspicacious analyst of the thorniest problems.

Franklin was also an attendee of their meetings during the years he spent in London—years during which I was obligated to converse with him more than once.

This club was notorious in its time—and, in certain circles, remains so—for its alleged orgiastic Satanic practices. I never observed anything of the sort, although the club was certainly populated by its share of libertines. Franklin himself was no stranger to the pleasures of the flesh and senses, but he possessed the common sense and fundamental goodwill (I struggle here to avoid enumerating his vices and infuriating personal qualities) to avoid an irreversible descent into debauchery. His interest in this secret club was the product of the same wellspring of curiosity and investigative spirit that gave rise to his other inquiries, be they the nature of electricity or the best methods by which men and women might learn to govern themselves. Such, at least, I believe from my meetings with the man. He, like General Washington, understood that the grand experiment of the American colonies foreshadowed the birth of a new species of government, and that the relocation of power from aristocrats and kings to commoners was more than a political maneuver. It was a new age in history, a decisive break from the past. However, when new ages dawn, the supernatural powers take note, for each new epoch brings opportunity for them as well. During periods of upheaval, demons strike and the heavenly powers are on guard. Such a time began in the 1770s and continues now.

The Freemasons understand such times. In the 1770s, they refashioned themselves as a band of outlaws—today the word *terrorist* would be applied to them, as it is applied to anyone, it seems, whose actions are motivated by a disagreeable politics. This transformation was led and overseen by General Washington himself, and it was he who set the Freemasons of the colonies their task of

collecting occult artifacts and other esoterica. Their power, even if poorly understood, was such that Washington put the highest priority on keeping them from the British. The ancient order, which had since its inception been deeply interested in lore and the knowledge of how things work—see their common emblem, the compass and square, by which great works are conceived, drawn, and erected—threw itself into these new missions with gusto. *Ordo ab Chao*—those words brought me into the Freemasons, and brought me eventually to General Washington himself. The belief in this creed is what turned me from a soldier of the Crown to a rebel filled with ideas about the rights of man, to borrow the clarion title of Thomas Paine's influential pamphlet—and to Paine goes all the credit. A great man he was. I learned to respect and admire the Volume of Sacred Writings (which was General Washington's Bible). I would not have become the man I am without the guidance of Freemasonry—and I say this knowing that men of the Masonic orders would kill me in a moment if they thought that act would further the commonweal.

[October 19]

I have just returned from a visit to what is known as an elementary school. As part of my "cover," Abigail has suggested I perform "outreach"—in other words, pretend to be a professor and speak to schools. This little masquerade is designed to allay the suspicions of some of Abigail's colleagues, who persist in viewing me as a suspect ("person of interest"—what a milquetoast phrase!) in the murders of not only Sheriff Corbin but everyone else who has run afoul of the Horseman and his minions.

The classrooms I visited are quite different from those in the schools I attended. They are brightly decorated, welcoming spaces, and the children are free within reason to move about and to speak. When I was eight years of age, we sat silently on benches and copied lessons, regurgitating them on command. I learned, oh yes, but it was only by some small miracle that I ever acquired any love of learning.

What a delight these modern schools turned out to be! The children were subject to many of the same errors and mythological understandings of their history that I noted on my first visit to the local historical society, but their eagerness and openness was a joy to me. I had continually to remind myself not to tell them too much of the truth—but is that not what all adults must consider in any conversation with a child too young to know of the world's darker truths?

These are the souls I most resolutely fight for. They deserve a world absent the dire threat of Moloch, and I will give that to them. They are sticky and noisy and unruly, and I love them without reservation.

Further notes on Moloch. Known to the ancients as a sun god—but not the life-giving sort akin to Ra. His were the sun's powers to sap the strength of men and kill them when they could not shelter from it. He was known as "prince of the valley of tears," after the location of his shrine in Tophet. The Greeks believed him an aspect of Cronus, who devoured his children—Moloch has power over time, perhaps? Is that another reason why he has taken an interest in me—my sojourn beyond the normal lifespan of a man? Medieval demonology held him to be especially pleased by the lamentations of mothers at the deaths of their children; it was also said that he was at his most powerful in autumn—the time when all things begin to die. Moloch steals children. He is always represented as having the head of a bull, or a bull calf.

I wonder, as I wander through this new age, what it might mean that demons are so much more easily encountered, their works so much more easily discerned, than those of angels. Does the tide of the battle between heaven and hell turn? Or have the angelic hosts chosen a path of action invisible to humans on Earth? If these first weeks reawakened from my long slumber have taught me nothing else, it is that one chooses either faith or despair. Because I have doubt, I am able to choose faith. The man who chooses despair rejects both doubt and faith.

Those around me—Abigail most prominently, but also Captain Irving, Jennifer, Henry Parish, even the Freemasons—they teach me. From them I choose to learn.

And now it has gotten quite late. One can only fight so much evil in one day. Before I sleep, I believe I will take another of those incredible hot showers. Abigail has suggested I might feel more at home in this time if I dressed as others do. This step I am not yet prepared to take. My skin is too accustomed to the touch of homespun and rough wool. I confess I look askance at the idea that so many of the garments now worn were created of materials called polyester and acrylic. These are apparently derived from plastic, which has become a noun in this time. I knew it previously only as an adjective describing an object without fixed shape or properties. The language goes on living, even when the speaker is magically asleep for two centuries and more.

This question of plastic is a complex one, apparently. I look around this cabin and see it everywhere. There are plastic containers of every shape, transparent or translucent or dyed with any color one might imagine. There are plastic bags for storage of food items, going by the moniker Ziploc—and where has the *K* gone from that name? "Branding," it seems, according to Abbie. One of the functions of this activity known as branding is the destruction of words in order that they may be formed into slogans. This age views language with deep suspicion and words as things that may be mutilated for the purpose of commerce. I am, it seems, quite old-fashioned by virtue of my habits of speech and writing—at least as much as by my dress.

Where my dress is concerned, I will continue as I have thus far. Soap and water are as much a wonder as the Internet or Ziploc bags. ("Baggies" they are called sometimes, following a strange tendency in this age to apply diminutives to everything. Mystifying.) Why would I fill a closet with clothing I do not want, when I keep my own clothes clean and they suit my preferences? A man can only bend so much to the winds of fashion.

[October 23]

The Horseman is ahead of us once again. He has located and murdered a number of the Freemasons, leaving their heads in Tarrytown's clock tower in a grotesque parody of the lanterns lit as a signal to Paul Revere—about whom more anon. The Horseman located his head and attacked the police laboratory where it was housed, killing the technician there and nearly doing away with Captain Irving, who fought off its invasion long enough to enable us to keep possession of the head. However, we have been unable to destroy it. Nothing in the guidance I have received from Katrina sheds any light on how this task might be accomplished. Irving, it must be added, is opposed to the idea of destroying the head, since he views it as evidence in several murder cases. He has been forced to confront the truth about the supernatural elements of our collective plight, of which he has until now been ruthlessly skeptical.

The Horseman also destroyed parts of a book belonging to the Freemasons, leading us to believe there is a way to destroy his head. The Freemasons knew of it, and the Horseman is out to ensure that even if we maintain physical possession of his skull, we will be doing little more than keeping it safe for him until he manages to wrest it from our dead hands.

———————

I have had occasion to do some reading while sequestered here in Corbin's cabin between hunting missions and responses to police emergencies. During the course of this reading, I was put in mind of Jonathan Swift—not his absurd *Gulliver's Travels* but his writing from a broadsheet called the *Examiner*: "Falsehood flies, and the truth comes limping after." I gather this phrase has been adapted (to put it politely) by a number of great minds who succeeded Swift as gadflies and blackly humorous commentators on human foolishness. Yet etymology, as fascinating as I find it ordinarily, is not my purpose here. I am thinking of the benevolent lies a people tells about itself, and more to the point I am thinking of the famous story of Paul Revere's midnight ride. *One if by land, two if by sea; and I on the opposite shore will be* . . . indeed. But the night in question was much more complex and dangerous than that little bit of doggerel suggests.

I was put in charge of protecting two fugitives from the Crown's justice, John Hancock and Samuel Adams—and again I pause to note the way certain "Founding Fathers" have entered the popular imagination. Hancock's was hardly the most embellished signature I ever saw, yet his signature has become the most famous in the history of this nation and his name a byword for the act of signing one's name: "Put your John Hancock there." It would perhaps be better if more Americans of this age knew their "Founding Fathers" as men rather than symbols. Adams was a brilliant and pugnacious man, uninterested in the malt houses from which his family earned their living, entirely devoted to ideals; his contribution to the American character comes from his steadfast Puritan idealism and his anger at the Crown. He was also mentor to Hancock, who was Adams's opposite in every respect. Scion of a rich mercantile family, lover of luxuries, and canny exploiter of loose shipping regulations, Hancock was the scintillating figurehead the American sentiment required. He and Adams argued, fiercely at times, but when their vision of America demanded it they were at each other's side. And so it was on the night of April 18, 1775, the occasion of Paul Revere's famous ride.

Revere is said to have been riding to warn the residents of Boston of an impending redcoat incursion. That would certainly have been part of his mission; it was well-known among us that recent British military aggression was soon to intensify. However, the primary aim of Revere's ride—and the cardinal reason for its timing and secrecy—was the transfer of a packet of intelligence. I saw it change hands from Adams to Revere before Revere left the safe house. I was told at the time that it contained secrets and inferred from this that Revere was to convey information about redcoat movements, troop strengths, and so forth. Upon seeing the package I noted with interest a symbol inscribed on its exterior. At the time I did not understand its significance, but I recall it as if I had only just observed Adams conveying it to Revere.

This heptagram, with its star-inside-a-star structure, was clearly a protective measure of some sort. Yet it was not until last night that I understood what I had seen. With Abigail's assistance I was guided to a file of Sheriff Corbin's and learned therein that this symbol is known as a Devil's Trap.

Revere, one must conclude, was carrying secret intelligence

vital to the war against the demonic legions rather than the soldiers of the Crown—although as my experience with Colonel Tarleton demonstrates, the two were at times one and the same.

I had occasion to speak with Revere after his ride, before the war drove us in different directions. He told the tale of pursuing redcoats, riding down his party and cutting them from their saddles one by one. This is one more event lost to the popular histories; I shall need an entirely different diary just to keep track of those! It is my deep suspicion—now, looking back on Revere's tale with the knowledge I have gained since—that the Hessian was among the pursuers, although Revere never said this and would have had no reason to specify. Further, since I have learned the meaning of the Devil's Trap, I now suspect the materials Revere delivered that night contained information on how the Horseman might be combated. His hanging of the heads in the clock tower now seems like a provocation. He wishes us to know what he knows; he wishes us to fear his apparent invulnerability. I, for my part, will fear him no more than is necessary to muster the courage I shall need to kill him.

On a lighter note: For all his Puritan dourness, Adams nurtured a love of off-color limericks. While I'm saddened that those he composed have been lost to history, I still amuse myself by crafting some of my own:

> The redcoats were chasing Revere
> With intentions warlike and severe
> But the harlots of Boston
> Tittered and caused 'em
> In another direction to veer.

Lord, let it never be said
That Hancock was easily led
If he spied women sweeter
He chose as his leader
Not the big, but the littler head.

Ten strumpets and ten trollops more
Besieged General Washington's door
He called them all in
To tell them their sin
And ended up adding one more!

And while I am amusing myself, a note on television. There is one in Sheriff Corbin's cabin, as I gather there is in nearly every American home—not to mention every waiting room, restaurant, tavern . . . they are so common I find myself surprised when I can turn in a complete circle and not see one. The televised plays—shows, they are called—are bewildering in their variety.

There is a thing called "science fiction," in which the most outlandish scenarios are treated as if they are real. My own situation is quite outlandish, viewed from the perspective of someone unaware of the dark conspiracies of Moloch and his acolytes, so perhaps I should not be peremptory in my assessment of these stories—yet how bizarre they are! Sentient beings from the distant reaches beyond the known planets; ships that can travel among the stars; the ingenuity of these movies makes them enjoyable.

Terrifying as well! In one, a parasite from a dead planet is taken aboard a ship and begins to hunt and kill the crew. I began watching this movie and found myself unable to look away. Then I, who have looked demons in the face and battled the minions of hell itself, was reluctant to extinguish the last light before I slept.

Perhaps I will refrain from mentioning this to Abigail, who doubtless would seize the opportunity to tease me mercilessly.

My resolve to remain silent about last night's fright evaporated as Abigail and I were in conversation. I told her of the movie, and my reaction to it. She laughed! Of course. I am quite amusing to her, and why not? To her, I am a character out of history, and my bafflement at what she finds ordinary is certain to be funny to her.

"That movie was called *Alien,* right?" she asked me. I nodded and she said, "That movie would scare Dracula. I never could watch it all the way through."

I made inquiries as to the identity of this Dracula, and now I have an entirely new set of fables to unnerve me. Vampires!? I had never heard of such things.

How these people love to terrify themselves!

We continued our investigations at the local historical society, where we were informed that the Revere manuscript was on loan to a military museum—in London, of all places. Its contents, however, were available "online."

And here I must digress.

The Internet. I believe I have begun to understand this strange, but seemingly important, hive of highly sophisticated calculating machines called "computers" that can also be used to store information by means of magnetism. One can access this vast storehouse of information by means of these machines, although learning those fiendish devices is a travail itself. I am doing so, but more slowly than I would like—and with the side effect of great hilarity on Abigail's part.

Fantastic. In the old sense of unbelievable, and yet it is commonplace here. Everyone seems to have this Internet even in their coat pockets, by means of "smartphones" that can access it. One wonders, then, why they are still called phones, or telephones, since my observations would indicate that few owners of these devices use them for telephonic communication.

I see children tapping on these phones to send each other messages when they are yards away from each other. It is as if the phone convinces its bearer that he exists in an entirely separate world, only accessible to the worlds of others by means of the device itself. The phone is a gatekeeper, sentry, jailer—all at once! If ever I possess one, I would hope that a friend—should I ever have a friend in this age—will end my life painlessly and with mercy.

Common phrases and expressions I find either fascinating, repellent, or simply of interest:

OMG

Sitting duck

Shooting fish in a barrel (one wonders if this phrase has an added meaning, for after all any barrel in which fish were shot would no longer hold water. . . .)

LOL

Catfish as verb

Game-changer

Impact as verb (abomination!)

Win-win

For the win

Boo-yah

Gridlock
Supermarket, superhighway, superstorm—everything must be super!
Noob, troll, spam . . . there are so many.

I have done it. Surmounting the obstacles we faced, I obtained a
paper copy of the Revere manuscript and immediately saw it was
a cipher. Adams was a partisan of a particular encryption method
now known as the Vigenère cipher—I used that name when
speaking of it to Abigail, because I assumed her police training
would have included at least the basics of cryptography, and took
care to brief myself on the terms now in use. In my time this construct was known as the polyalphabetic cipher of Giovan Battista
Bellaso, for it was only later—while I lay in the cave under the
spells of my beloved Katrina—that it was misattributed to Blaise
de Vigenère.

The fundamental principle of the Vigenère cipher is multiple
layers of substitution. A simple code is easily broken if one has any
grasp of the relative frequencies with which different letters occur
in the message's language. In English, the most common letter is E,
followed by T and A. Once the positions of those are established,
the rest of the content may be deduced with ease. The difficulty is
multiplied infinitely by the introduction of a second key, a phrase
overlaid on the first cipher that changes the substitution with each
letter. Without knowing the key, it is nearly impossible to grasp the
underlying pattern of the cipher. I wrestled in vain with the coded
passage, trying a number of keys—*Washington, Adams, Hancock,
Revere,* various others—until in a moment of frustration I glanced
over at the Horseman's skull and saw something unusual. Sunlight
from the archive's high windows was now, late in the day, striking
the skull at a different angle, revealing that the skull's teeth were

inlaid with silver. On that silver were etched letters: CICERO.

In that moment I knew this must be the key.

Who had done this? Someone had taken possession of the Hessian's head, reduced it to bone, and left this message. Undoubtedly a circuitous route to follow if one wished to communicate a code key, but it made as much sense as any other method given the circumstance. The visionary who had left this message had known that a future confrontation with the Horseman loomed, and knew too that the knowledge of how he might be fought would be lost over the centuries. I suppose, seeing the material of the inlay was silver, that Paul Revere himself—a silversmith by trade—performed the task. If so, all Americans have yet another reason to be grateful to him.

Why Cicero? I can only speculate that Revere chose this key in honor of the Roman orator's belief in republican ideals. He was a defender of Rome against the constant encroachment of tyranny—though I suspect he would consider the United States, with its numerous representative bodies and constant bickering, an undisciplined rabble. One must always be wary of ascribing to the ancients ideals more at home in this modern age.

Cicero was also the pen name chosen by Arthur Bernard, whose pamphlets Revere would have read. Perhaps he also knew Bernard personally. I cannot help but believe that both Revere and Bernard drew on the legacy of Ciceronian thought: Bernard to disguise himself, and Revere to unlock the secrets of the Horseman's vulnerability. What tangled webs we weave.

VPGLFF UMOEEO DPQVJH JMTEUW CVEIFT
UWNMKW UPKWNS CSPIJG JMEEEB QBDIYS

NLHSIS XMTAYC YWWPUG GQBIYW OCUIKV
KAUMXW NIFIMW NAVVRD CVFQLG VNKRUO
YQVGYK JWOEPA CSGPLB CWHWFZ IE

I write the Vigenère cipher thus, broken into six-letter groups, because the key CICERO consists of six letters. W, the first letter, corresponds to the first C in CICERO. C is the third letter of the alphabet—or two moves from the letter A—so the V has been advanced two places from the actual letter. In other words, for that letter, V equals T. Next, P, which corresponds to the I in CICERO. I being eight moves from A, that P must be moved back eight places in the alphabetic order—yielding H. And so forth. Continuing, one finds (with correct word breaks and a guess at intended punctuation):

THE HORSEMAN ABHORS THE RADIANCE
OF SOL. IT IS HIS WEAKNESS. HE CANNOT BE
HELD FOREVER; WHO WOULD SEIZE HIM USE
THIS SIGIL, A DEVIL'S TRAP—AND MUST FIND A
WITCH WHO MAY MAKE LUNA OF SOL. GW

Thus I broke the cipher and went to find Abigail—who was deep in conversation with the revenant Brooks. I write those words as if the occasion was nothing unusual, and indeed given other recent events a casual conversation with an undead man is barely worth notice. Brooks was wracked with guilt over his complicity in the Horseman's actions, and agreed to convey a message that the Horseman should meet us at the clock tower at nightfall.

Abigail, naturally, demanded to know why I sought a direct engagement with the Horseman. Showing her my scrawled decryption of the manuscript, I explained the outlines of my plan. The Horseman of Death cannot be captured, but he can be trapped—thus the Devil's Trap on the packet Revere carried. His weakness is sunlight, which we would have inferred from his nocturnal attacks thus far even if Katrina had not told me as much weeks ago, and to trap him, a witch must be found who can work a spell to transform the sun into the moon. This seemed a metaphor to me at the time, and I still am indecisive as to its true meaning.

Tonight will tell. We have gathered the materials we need and all that remains is to wait for night.

Regna terrae, cantate Deo, psallite Domino qui fertis super caelum caeli ad Orientem
Ecce dabit voci Suae vocem virtutis, tribuite virtutem Deo.

Exorcizamus te, omnis immundus spiritus omnis satanica potestas, omnis incursio infernalis adversarii, omnis legio, omnis congregatio et secta diabolica.

Ergo draco maledicte et omnis legio diabolica adjuramus te.
Cessa decipere humanas creaturas, eisque aeternae Perditionis venenum propinare.

Vade, Satana, inventor et magister omnis fallaciae, hostis humanae salutis.
Humiliare sub potenti manu dei, contremisce et effuge, invocato a nobis sancto et terribili nomine, quem inferi tremunt.

Ab insidiis diaboli, libera nos, Domine.
Ut Ecclesiam tuam secura tibi facias libertate servire, te rogamus, audi nos.
Ut inimicos sanctae Ecclesiae humiliare digneris, te rogamus, audi nos.
Ut inimicos sanctae Ecclesiae te rogamus, audi nos.

Terribilis Deus de sanctuario suo.
Deus Israhel ipse truderit virtutem et fortitudinem plebi Suae.
Benedictus Deus. Gloria Patri.

—An exorcism

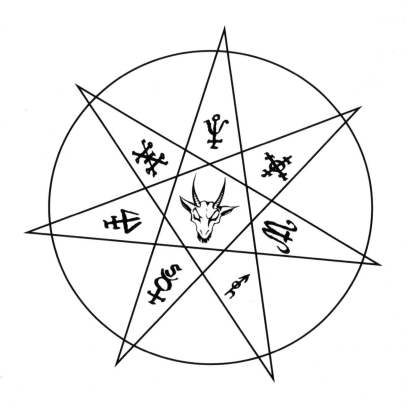

While we pass the time, I write in this journal and Abigail unburdens herself. She left the archive earlier to speak with a former paramour, the officer Luke, whose hostility toward me is now understandable, if still misplaced. Reaching for the only example I had, I told Abigail that despite the course of events I would change nothing about my love for Katrina. Her mystery and allure came at the cost of secrecy; I understand this now, and would have it no other way. This appeared to change Abigail's mind about something. She has left again to speak to Luke.

Consideration of matters of the heart always returns me to thoughts of Katrina. We stole a few days together once, shortly after our marriage, when it was clear that the tides of the war to come would draw us apart more often than permit us any time together. The locale was a cabin on the banks of the Potomac, let to us by General Washington as a wedding gift. We had wed without benefit of family presence, either mine or hers—mine due to my father's vehement opposition to the union, and hers due to an estrangement from her relations whose origin and nature she was reluctant to discuss. Looking back with the aid of what I now know of her membership in the Radiant Heart, I can only suspect that the familial discord stemmed from her family's disapproval— yet I do not know that for sure.

I recall the rhododendrons in full flower on the grounds, and have had a fondness for that plant ever since. Those were the finest days of my life. There was nothing in the world save we two, in the first full bloom of love. I looked upon Katrina with wonder, scarcely able to believe she had assented to my proposal. One always wonders, I suppose, whether the meeting of minds and hearts in marriage will be as beautiful in the event as it has been in the imagination beforehand—and for us it surely was. We took such joy in each other's company that when we took our leave from the cabin and plunged back into the cause of the colonies' independence, we were both incalculably stronger for the knowledge that neither of us would ever face troubled times alone. Remembering those days was a source of strength to me during the most difficult and dangerous moments of the war. I fought not just for the independence of the infant United States of America, but for a return to my beloved Katrina and for the peace that would permit us to build our lives together as we both wished.

I wonder what has become of the letters I wrote her, and she wrote to me. Mine are doubtless gone to rot on the battlefield along the banks of the creek running into the Hudson, where the Horseman and I struck each other down. Perhaps she saved them? I cannot imagine how, so pressing were her circumstances. Should I ever encounter those letters again, I will consider it a great gift from the Infinite.

What pleasure this memory brings, for it is she I fight for—and when she is free, we will continue the fight by each other's sides. She was a witch? Very well, she was a witch. Perhaps she even enchanted me into falling in love with her with the flowers that always seemed to be in her hair. Again, very well; for my love has long since overpowered whatever charm she might have mustered. It is mine, and hers, and its magic is only the magic of two hearts meeting and becoming one.

Also: In honor of our nuptials, a mystery poet—though I have my suspicions about the source—sent a few more bawdy lines of verse:

> Ichabod Crane is to ride
> On an errand with Mohawks for guides
> Pursuing the Hessian

He must not stop to freshen
His mood with Katrina his bride.

Now, remembering that little bit of poesy, I cannot help but
wonder if it was my friend John Adams having one more sly joke
than I had previously understood. I fought many Hessians during
the war, but he would have known the degree of their complicity in
the occult maneuverings to which I was as yet a stranger. Whoever
the sender, I cannot but toast the sharp tooth of your wit.

———————————

That damned limerick has guided my thoughts along prurient
lines. Since I am the only one who will read this—unless I am
dead, in which case it will no longer matter—I confess in these
pages that I have encountered the, shall we say, less salutary pre-
cincts of the Internet. I will not commit details to paper; however,
I will say I long for Katrina yet more intensely after this inadver-
tent journey through the fleshly cornucopia of these sites. Our
union was ever a healthy one. (I am put reluctantly in mind of yet
another pompous aphorism from the pen of Franklin, who once
wrote, "Rarely use venery but for health or offspring"—yet I do
not think I reveal any harmful secrets when I say that he was a
devotee of the physical pleasures to a degree exceeding that necessary for health.) Katrina and I would have had children one day;
we certainly had adequate practice to ensure the process would go
smoothly.

———————————

The Horseman is trapped! Using a cell deep in the tunnels where
the Freemasons created a supernatural barrier long ago, and a
large number of electric lamps whose light shines on the same

wavelengths as the invisible portion of the sun's rays—*ultraviolet* is the term Abigail used—we drew the Horseman from the clock tower into the tunnels, guiding him into our trap with a trail of skulls. Compelled to touch each skull to discern whether it was his, the Horseman walked straight into our snare.

Now the question is: How long can we hold him? For surely his supernatural allies will rally to his rescue.

[October 29]

The enemy has begun his counteroffensive, striking deep at the most crucial element of any soldier's arsenal: belief in the rightness of his cause.

We had the Horseman, and we required a means to communicate with him, for a prisoner is of little use when he cannot be interrogated. The first possibility that suggested itself to me was Brooks, who had demonstrated some sympathy for Abigail and me the night before—and who had demonstrated the ability to communicate with the Horseman by means of necromancy.

Brooks had last been seen in the tunnels, so it was there we sought him again. It took little time to locate his hiding place, where he had brought a box of ephemera from his mortal life: photographs, papers, mementos. The area was also quite liberally festooned with necromantic images, leading me to believe that Brooks was the ideal method by which we might communicate not just with the Hessian, but with Moloch himself. Many of the symbols I observed, inscribed by Brooks's own hand, were ancient in origin and hearkened back to the Egyptians, who first advanced the practice of communing with the dead beyond its shamanistic origins.

When confronted, Brooks made no secret of his powers. He

was quite unwilling to let himself be used as a conduit for communication with the Horseman, but I stood firm despite Abigail's misgivings.

As events were shortly to teach me, this was a headstrong stance and one I should have reconsidered. I goaded the Horseman into using Brooks to speak, thinking I could pry from him the secrets of his origin and power. Instead, I received a sharp and painful lesson in the unintended consequences of decisions made in the heat of emotion.

For the Horseman is no Hessian at all, but the walking corpse of Abraham Van Brunt. My friend, my rival in love, and now my immortal enemy. It was he to whom Katrina was initially betrothed, he whom she left to become my wife in 1775—and he whom I was forced to abandon to the redcoats. Forced, I say, because even knowing what I now know, I am still unable to discern what I might have done differently.

Despite our friendship, I was not blind to Van Brunt's flaws. He was a stalwart ally, a brave soldier, and also a vain and arrogant man who had captured Katrina through an arrangement between their families. He was devoted to her in his way, however, and I accompanied him to a jeweler's once to help him purchase a necklace in celebration of their engagement. True to his nature, he settled on the most ornate piece the jeweler had on offer, but I dissuaded him, suggesting that a simpler piece was more in keeping with Katrina's character. He bestowed it upon her later, at a gathering of influential colonists sympathetic to the cause of liberty—though it was a social occasion and politics were discussed with great discretion, since the guest list included loyalists as well. Katrina caught my eye when Abraham gave her the necklace, and as if we both had the gift of mind reading I could see her certainty that I had in fact selected the gift.

Later she came to me and said she intended to break off her engagement to Abraham. After she did so—with, I insist, no encouragement on my part—he naturally was humiliated, and genuinely heartbroken as well; it would have suited both of us if we had never again had cause to interact. Events are rarely so amenable to the wishes of their participants, however, and we were charged with a vital mission: to deliver the Declaration and Resolves to the First Continental Congress, then about to convene in Philadelphia. This document was the ancestor of the more justly renowned Declaration of Independence, which in turn could not have existed had not the leaders of the colonies had an earlier document to use as a sounding board. It clarified their goals and beliefs while also forging a consensus on articles whose proposal was met with resistance.

As Abraham and I rode, my guilty conscience overmastered my powers of tact, and I confessed to him the love Katrina and I shared. This was the right action, perhaps, but taken at the wrong time—he grew enraged and drew his sword. I fought him, pleading the while that he put up his sword and listen to reason—but before his temper could cool he was struck by a bullet and fell. The redcoats approached and I was faced with a terrible decision. I had not the time to minister to him, and 'twas unthinkable to let the Declaration of Resolves fall into British hands before it could be announced under the imprimatur of the Continental Congress. Duty to country—for so we already believed the colonies to be, de facto if not de jure—outweighed duty to friend. I fled, evading the redcoats, and fulfilled my mission, though I left Abraham to die.

I spoke of this to Abigail, as she learned that the Hessians in the present day had broken into an antiquities merchant and stolen an object known as the Thracian Phiale. This item was a powerful focus of magic, and in conjunction with certain incantations could be used to break the enchantment holding the Horseman shackled in the cell Jefferson built.

The mind reels at times, considering the number and variance of magical traditions being brought to bear in this war. Egyptian and Greek, European and Native American—and Druidic, as I was soon to learn from Jennifer. It was she who gave us to understand that the Thracian Phiale was not Greek at all, but a creation of Druidic sects who receded into hiding after the Christianization of Britain. They passed their traditions through secret writings, some of which Miss Jenny had come across while hunting for artifacts. The Phiale would disrupt the Horseman's imprisonment if we did not take immediate measures to prevent its use, she warned—but again I was too headstrong to listen. I would not wait for help, because we had already opened the interrogation, with Brooks as intermediary, and the Horseman had already produced the very necklace I selected for Katrina two hundred years and more before this day. I demanded the truth from him as our enemies approached from all sides—and from within.

DRUIDS. *Sorcerous sect of pre-Roman Celtic origin. Suppressed by Romans, later by Christianization. Latin* druides *or* druidae, *contemporary with Greek* δρυΐδης—*both traceable to older Irish and Welsh* drui/dryw, *"seer" or "sorcerer." Almost nothing is known reliably of their practices, though they are an eternally fecund source of myth and facile nature worship. Likely connected to the oak tree, which due to its longevity and strength was held to be a repository of wisdom.*

The Hessians had appealed to Moloch for assistance, and they received it. Hessian fighters cut off the electricity to the building, turning off the ultraviolet lamps. At the same time, a demonic beast, the likes of which I have never seen and pray never to see again, tore through the police guard and forced its way through the tunnels, where the Horseman was freeing himself of the shackles now that the ultraviolet lamps no longer sapped his strength. Brooks, taking advantage of our distraction, disgorged the Thracian Phiale from his body, and we understood too late that his show of sympathy to our cause was merely a ruse; it had taken us in completely. We were now soon to confront the Horseman restored to his powers.

Sensing his advantage, the Horseman spoke through Brooks again, taunting me, telling me that he had traded his soul to achieve his fondest wish: Katrina. In a flash I understood: Moloch held Katrina captive because the promise of her holds the Horseman in his sway.

The only reason I survived to write this is a final intervention from Brooks—who, as the Horseman raised his weapon to strike me down and achieve the goal for which he had suffered so long, stayed his hand. Hessian acolytes spirited the Horseman away, and Brooks as well, using the darkness as cover while I strengthened.

The inference is clear and unmistakable: Moloch does not wish me dead. Now that our blood has been separated by the Sin Eater Henry Parish, Van Brunt could have killed me tonight but did not. As long as Moloch holds Katrina, Van Brunt will do his bidding. What do we do with this knowledge? How am I to cope with knowing that my wife is a demon's prize? And how to turn that knowledge into action—and into victory?

The key is to know why Moloch wishes to preserve my life. With that information we may begin to concoct a plan to turn Moloch's own goals against him—and use the Horseman as the linchpin of that turning.

I slept little last night. The thought of Katrina in her forest Purgatory, subject to the demonic whim of Moloch himself—what man could sleep?

Also the question of betrayal prevented my eyes from closing and my mind from taking rest. An ugly word, *betrayal.* From the Latin *tradere,* "to hand over." Did I hand Abraham Van Brunt over to our mutual enemies?

Unquestionably I did. But could I have done otherwise? Had I stayed to fight, and both of us been killed, British discovery of the Declaration and Resolves would have endangered a number of the delegates to the Continental Congress. Apart from the loss of life, surely it would have delayed the independence of the colonies from Britain, perhaps for decades.

Against that knowledge, I weigh the memory of leaving Van Brunt behind . . . and though just yesterday I wrote of the necessity of choosing reason over emotion, in this case I find myself unable to make that choice. For without the staying hand of emotion, reason turns the human mind into a calculating machine—one more node, perhaps, in the Internet. There is no worse fate for a mind that believes itself capable of independent thought, or a heart that yearns for the love of fellow creatures, including my Masonic brethren who have been murdered by the Hessian.

I have not written of it these past few days because my instinct would have been to indulge in self-pity—that weakest and most despicable of vices! They are gone. They would have killed me, but they were true brothers, and perhaps the nearest thing I might have had to true friends (Abigail apart). Our side in this war is inestimably weakened by their loss. I would reach out to other Freemasons in and around Sleepy Hollow, but not all of the brethren are initiated into the deeper mysteries; not all possess the darkest secrets; that is as it should be, yet it makes any contact difficult. I must wait until events demand such a desperate embassy—or until others within Freemasonry reach out to me. You are out there, my brothers; I know it. But where? Make yourselves known, I beg of you.

———————

I am probably not, as they say, in the spirit of this holiday called Halloween. When I saw a small child dressed as a witch—or as the Headless Horseman, of whom I counted four today, none more than ten years of age—I immediately ran to Abigail and warned her that the Order of the Blood Moon was openly asserting its diabolical powers and drawing innocent children into their coven. How she laughed!

There was a Hallowmas celebration in the England of my youth, but it consisted primarily of groups of drunken young men singing rowdy songs and demanding gifts from their more sedate neighbors in return for the promise of prayers for the dead. How it became the province of children I know not, although it seems unsurprising that a celebration involving costumes and sweets would draw children in. Samhain, the ancient Celtic holiday, lies behind it all—that time when the boundary between the worlds of the living and the dead was thinnest and most permeable. In America it has all been buried under a tide of festival good cheer. I suspect the spirits, accustomed as they were to a certain amount of deference, are quite irritated by this development.

A few thoughts that remain on my mind:

- Miss Jenny is proving herself an invaluable asset. She has knowledge of the secret undercurrents of Sleepy Hollow, thanks to her work on behalf of Sheriff Corbin—and she also has a soldier's nature. By that I mean that she is the type of person (I almost wrote man) who constantly feels the lack of battle whenever there is no battle to fight. She throws herself into combat with both gusto and intelligence. We will need her in the future, perhaps more than we have already needed her thus far.

- I have been doing a bit of reading in the imaginative literature of this country. Fascinating—I find Twain a splendid raconteur. Also I happened to pick up a volume by William Faulkner. His language is by turns intoxicating and opaque, but one senses every word was carefully placed. I must read more of him before I decide whether he is a literary experimentalist or a purveyor of glib nonsense masquerading as emotional profundity.

- In addition to his dalliance with slaves (which I reflexively denied when Abigail first mentioned it, but now I have come to understand that it is established fact), Jefferson possessed an inordinate fondness for puns—not a transgression on the order of adultery, certainly, but another facet of him that he angled away from public view. The Founding Fathers (this is a source of constant surprise for those who did not know them as men) were like anyone else, with a full human array of foibles and peccadilloes.

[November 3]

I was approached today by a man dressed in colonial garb and festooned with buttons signifying his allegiance to various candidates standing in tomorrow's election. After the recent Halloween celebration, I had grown used to seeing people in costume on the streets of Sleepy Hollow. I was not prepared, however, for his boisterous proclamation that he was a member of the Tea Party. Since I was present at the original event of that name and did not recognize him as a fellow visitor from the past—one never knows these days—I inquired what in fact his Tea Party might be. He returned that it was a conservative group, allied with but not beholden to the Republican Party. I then asked what that might be—for the Founding Fathers, Washington in particular, were mortally opposed to political parties and envisioned the political structure of the new republic in a way expressly intended to avoid their institution. It seems their efforts were in vain, for now there are Democrats and Republicans, and no candidate refusing affiliation with one of those stands any chance of election . . . with, apparently, rare exceptions at which my Tea Party interlocutor scoffed with great vigor.

The history of this so-called Tea Party stems from frustration over taxation. *Plus ça change!* Yet this Tea Partier appeared most concerned with the intrusion of government into his private life. This is a worry most certainly shared by the Founding Fathers, but I'm not sure that they ever could have imagined the world we now live in. . . .

Tomorrow is Election Day. I am drinking coffee in a shop

devoted to that divine bean—at two dollars per cup!—and listening to people make entreaties to people just outside. However, many display no interest. How can this be? In a land where everyone may shout his opinion on the street, what possible reason could there be for not seizing the opportunity to make that opinion known by secret ballot? One that so many of my brothers and I died on the battlefield for?

Abigail's answer to this question was succinct and, I fear, cynical: She shrugged and said most people did not believe their votes made any difference. Astonishing! What else can make a difference? I shall never understand Americans.

That said, the Tea Partier's tricorn hat was quite dignified. Not all men can wear them well. Katrina used to prefer me in less formal haberdashery.

The Spanish influence on this country is quite extraordinary. I knew little of it when I was present in the Colonies, beyond an understanding that Spanish missionaries were active in the Floridas and in the west beyond the Mississippi River. But to look at a map of this country is to see the Hispanophone influence writ large: Tejas now Texas, Colorado, Nevada, Arizona, Montana, New Mexico (!)—and the burgeoning cities of Los Angeles, San Francisco, San Diego, San Antonio. How holy this vision of the Spanish America must have been . . . although from what I understand of Las Vegas, the piety of the missionary Franciscans has been replaced by quite a different way of life.

We hold these truths to be self-evident:

- *That "leftenant" is an intrinsically superior pronunciation;*
- *That buttons are in all cases superior to zippers;*
- *That cotton and wool are in all cases superior to artificial fabrics;*
- *That books should be composed of pages which can be turned rather than screens to be swiped;*
- *That it is no dishonor to be termed "old-fashioned";*
- *That contemporary modes of feminine dress are to be saluted, and those of male dress to be eyed skeptically;*
- *That urban life in these United States would be much improved by the re-introduction of horses;*
- *That it was a grave error on the part of the Framers to omit privacy from their enumerated list of natural rights;*
- *That it was a yet graver error on their part to make no clear provision eliminating chattel slavery;*
- *That despite that and other errors, the founding documents of this country are marvels of vision and endurance;*
- *That this future is good and I consider myself quite privileged to experience it.*

[November 7]

I continue to be fascinated by Sheriff Corbin's meticulous files, which yield countless curiosities . . .

ENVOIS DE ROME. Saint Remy di... ...élève de 4e année.

OFFICE OF THE WESTCHESTER COUNTY MEDICAL EXAMINER

88 Hudson Street
Sleepy Hollow, NY 10599

REPORT OF INVESTIGATION BY COUNTY MEDICAL EXAMINER

DECEDENT: **SADIE** **PAIGE** **BARTON** RACE **W** SEX **F** AGE **25**

First Name   Middle Name   Last Name

HOME ADDRESS: **801 IRVING DR.** .... MWSD OCCUPATION: **PA.**

TYPE OF DEATH: Violent ☐   Casualty ☐   Suicide ☐   Suddenly when in apparent health ☐   Found Dead **☒**
In Prison ☐   Suspicious, unusual or unnatural ☐   Cremation ☐

Comment ....

If Motor Vehicle Accident Check One: Driver ☐   Passenger ☐   Pedestrian ☐   Unknown ☐
Notification by **J. DeRose** .... Address **1809 Sleepy Hollow Dr.**
Investigating Agency **SHPD**

Description of Body   Clothed **☒**   Unclothed ☐   Partly Clothed ☐

Eyes **GREEN**   Hair **RED**   Mustache **N/A**   Beard **N/A**

Weight **106** Pounds   Length ____ Feet Inches   Body Temp ____ Farenheit   Date and Time **7/15 0800**

Rigor: Yes **☒**   No ☐   Lysed ☐   Liver Color ____ Fixed ☐   Non-Fixed ☐

Marks and Wounds ....

Victim choked on vomit

PROBABLE CAUSE OF DEATH	MANNER OF DEATH	DISPOSITION OF CASE
Choking	*(check one only)* Accident ☐ Natural **☒** Suicide ☐ Unknown **☒** Homicide ☐ Pending ☐	1. Not a medical examiner case ☐ 2. Autopsy requested Yes **☒** No ☐ Autopsy ordered Yes **☒** No ☐ Pathologist **Dr. Treiber**

I hereby declare that after receiving notice of the death described herein I took charge of the body and made inquiries regarding the cause of death in accordance with Section 21-830-33-69(b) Massachusetts Code Annotated and that the information contained herein regarding such death is true and correct to the best of my knowledge and belief.

7/15/11   **Sleepy Hollow**   *Whitby Lodge*
Date   Place of Investigation   Signature of County Medical Examiner

STATE OF NEW YORK
APPLICATION FOR PERMIT TO
CARRY CONCEALED FIREARMS
(Resident)

_____ NEW ($75.00)
_____ RENEWAL ($50.00)
_____ CHANGE OF ADDRESS ($10.00)

FOR OFFICE USE ONLY
CHECK #: **6969** LICENSE #:
___ $75.00 ___ $50.00 ___ $10.00
X ISSUE ___ DENIED DATE:
EXPIRATION DATE (IF ISSUED)
KNOWLEDGE OF HANDGUN SAFETY:

FULL NAME (First, Middle, Last)

Chaswick Clinard

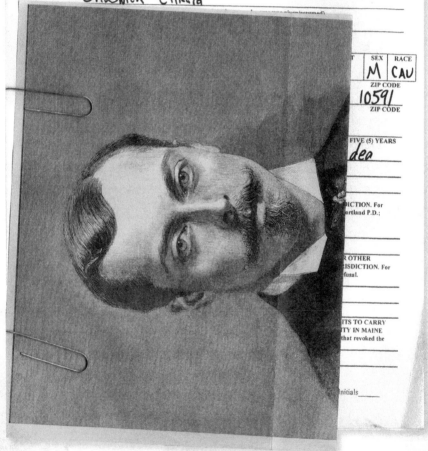

SEX	RACE
M	CAU

ZIP CODE
10591
ZIP CODE

FIVE (5) YEARS
deo

DICTION. For
ortland P.D.;

R OTHER
ISDICTION. For
fusal.

ITS TO CARRY
TY IN MAINE
that revoked the

Initials ____

OFFICE OF THE WESTCHESTER COUNTY MEDICAL EXAMINER
88 Hudson Street
Sleepy Hollow, NY 10599

Case N°.

MEDICAL EXAMINER

RACE W SEX F AGE 26

S D OCCUPATION: Secretary

in apparent health ☐ Found Dead ☒

emation ☐

rian ☐ Unknown ☐

cle Street

Partly Clothed ☐

N/A Beard N/A

p Date and Time 6/1/13 1:00am
Farenheit

Normal Fixed ☐ Non-Fixed ☐

DISPOSITION OF CASE

t a medical examiner case

topsy requested Yes ☐ No ☐

topsy ordered Yes ☐ No ☐

thologist

ook charge of the body and made inquiries
ssachusetts Code Annotated and that the
best of my knowledge and belief.

Whitby Lodge
Signature of County Medical Examiner

L'ILLUSTRATION, JOURNAL UNIVERSEL.

FOUILLES DE M. BEULÉ A CARTHAGE, Ruines des fortifications puniques de Byrsa.

159

LE GÉNIE DU COMPAGNONNAGE FAISANT LE TOUR DU GLOBE.

herren stig auch auff in der stain. Da das heer
geschen manne vñ sein haussfrawe. sy vielen ni=
der geneygt an die erd vñ fürbas erschine yn
mimer der engel des herrē.vñ er sprach zu sei=
ner haussfrawen. Wir werdē sterben des todes
wañ wir haben geschē den herren. Das weybe
antwurt im.Ob vns der herre wolt erschlahen
er hette nit empfange das gätz opfer.vnd dye
opfer vō vnsern hende.Noch hette vns gezey=
get alse dise ding.noch hette vns gesagt sy dise

die da sein künfftig. Darumb sy gepar einē sun
vñ hieß seinē name sampsō. Vñ dz kind wuchs
vnd der herre gesegent im.vñ der geyst des her
ren begund zusein in im . in den herbergen dan
zwischen saraa vñ esthaol

¶ **Das.XIIII.Capitel. wie**
sampson ein weyb name vñ auff dem weg einē
lewen tödet.vnd do er widerkame wie yne das
weyß betrog.

ARüB sampson gieg
ab in thammata . vnd sah da ein weyb
von den töchtern der philistiner . vnd
gieng auff.vnd verkunt es seine vater. vnd sey=
ner muter.sagend. Ich hab geschē ein weyb in
thammata von den töchtern der philistiner .ich
bitt euch das ir mir es gebet zu einē weyb.Der
vater.vnd sein muter sprachen zu in . Ist dann
keyn weyb vnder den töchtern deyner brüder.
vnd vnder allem volck.das du wolt nemē
ein weyb vō dē philistinern.Sy da sei enbeschni=
ten.Vñ sampson sprach zu seinē vater . Nyme
mir dise.wañ sy gefelt meine auge. wañ sein va
ter [...] muter westen nit das das ding wz
[...] vnd suchet die schulde wider sy
[...] der selben zeit herschete Sy
[...]el. Darüb sampson gieng
[...] mit der muter in tham=
[...] kumen zu dem weyn=

geyst des herren viel auff sampson. vnd er zer=
risse dē lewe zu stücken.als zerrisse er ein kitz=
len.vnd het gantz nichts in der hande.vnd ditz
wolte er nicht sagen dem vater oder der muter
Vnd gieng ab.vnd redet zu dem weybe. sy da
geviel seinen augen . Vnd nach etlichen tagen
keret er wid das er sy nem.Er neygt sich.das er
sehe das aß des lewen. Vnd sehe ein schwarm d
bienen.was in seynem munde. vnd ein rosen des
hönigs.Da er es het genomen in yhe hende.er
aß an dem weg.vnd kum zu seynem vater vñ zu
der muter. vnd gab in einen teyl.vnd sye assen.
Jedoch er wolt in es nit sagen . das er hett geno=
nomen das hönig von dem mund des lewen.
Darumb sein vater gieng ab zu dem weybe.vñ
machet eyn wirtschafft mit seinz sun sampson
Als die jungen hette gewonheit zu thun. Dar=
umb da in die burger der statt hetten gesehen.
sy gaben im dreyssig gesellen die da waren mit

Terenti' cu
Directorio
Glofa iterlineali
Cométarijs
Vocabuloru
Sententiaru
auis Comice
Donato
Gvidone
Afcenfio

EORVNDEM
CASTRORVM
DISPOSITIO, MVNDVM
referens, & Templum.

Genes. 48. ỹ. 5. & Cap. 49. ỹ. 4. 7. 9. 13. 14. 17. 19. 21. Deut. 33. ỹ. 26.

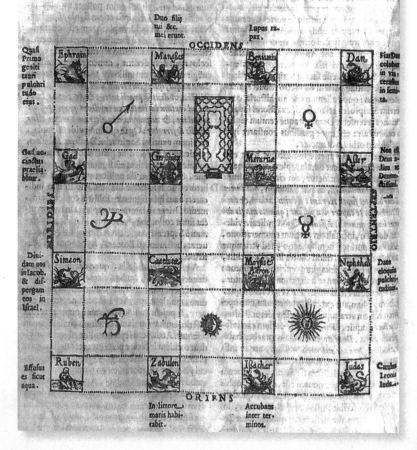

A word about this upcoming Thanksgiving holiday. Several words, in fact.

The colonies proclaimed a day of thanksgiving so frequently that one might encounter a feast at any moment wherever one went. A good harvest, a return from a dangerous voyage, a stretch of fine weather after a storm, or a welcome rain after a drought—all of these at various times provided the impetus for a day of feasting and prayer.

I myself carried a draft of a Thanksgiving declaration to the town of York, Pennsylvania, in 1777 while the British occupied Philadelphia and the Continental Congress was forced to a temporary home. Samuel Adams drafted it. It read in part:

> It is therefore recommended to the legislative or executive Powers of these United States to set apart Thursday, the eighteenth Day of December next, for Solemn Thanksgiving and Praise: That at one Time and with one Voice, the good People may express the grateful Feelings of their Hearts, and consecrate themselves to the Service of their Divine Benefactor; and that, together with their sincere Acknowledgments and Offerings, they may join the penitent Confession of their manifold Sins, whereby they had forfeited every Favor; and their humble and earnest Supplication that it may please God through the Merits of Jesus Christ, mercifully to forgive and blot them out of Remembrance . . .

[I redact some, for Adams was quite verbose at times—this is ever the vice of the politician, is it not?]

And it is further recommended, That servile Labor, and such Recreation, as, though at other Times innocent, may be unbecoming the Purpose of this Appointment, be omitted on so solemn an Occasion.

I gather Washington issued another proclamation in 1789—this from the Internet, which, God save me, I am beginning to turn to as a useful source of information on the two centuries I passed in enchanted slumber. But this was the first national proclamation of which I am aware, and I must say it contrasts quite violently with the spectacle of Thanksgiving as seen today.

Firstly, anyone who has ever attempted to hunt a wild turkey with such firearms as the Plymouth colonists possessed will know that success in that endeavor is entirely dependent on the will of the Great Architect of the Universe, those weapons being so inaccurate that one might well miss a turkey while it peered down the barrel. A feast for the entire population could hardly have depended on the presence of adequate turkey. The meal would have been venison, and cod, and eels, and other more easily taken birds, such as doves and partridges. If the colonists had any chickens, they certainly would have found their way to the table as well. There would have been corn and some grains. If anyone had solved the mystery of making cranberries palatable, perhaps there would have been a sauce of cranberries, as I understand is now traditional. But the occasion would not have marked harmony with the Indians, although they were certainly invited to that legendary feast.

Secondly, the Thanksgiving proclamation of Adams expressly disavowed servile labor and frivolous recreation. So what does one do on Thanksgiving now, in 2013? One eats to stupefaction while watching so-called football—the most frivolous of recreations—while one is bombarded by television advertisements for discounted commercial goods, in preparation for shopping excursions that would not be possible without servile labor. Arrant madness.

And what is this Black Friday? They speak of shopping as if it is a dark ritual, a holy occasion whose observance far outstrips the more homely imperatives of sharing food and drink with those one loves. At midnight they stream to their shopping malls, like congregants at a Church of Commerce, taking the communion of sales. I confess a contrary impulse to buy nothing, to remain in my own clothes, patching and mending them as necessary, solely that I might not be converted to quasi-religious madness. Yet even in the midst of my private jeremiad, I also find myself infernally attracted to the spectacle!

But Abigail is here. Perhaps she will take me shopping . . . although I fear that once we have entered a mall, she will be relentless in imploring me to change my comfortable clothes for contemporary styles. More anon.

[November 24]

An eventful day yesterday. Once again I returned to a location I knew well from my previous life, and once again that return had unexpected consequences. On this occasion the location was Fredericks Manor, a house I knew as a result of my friendship with Lachlan Fredericks. A grand man, Lachlan. Irish to the core, a lover of food and drink and humanity. His house was a way station and refuge for all in need of shelter and protection, whatever their creed or color. Abigail and I were called to Fredericks Manor to investigate the disappearance of its new owner, a billionaire—one woman with a billion dollars! The colonies' collective wealth in 1780 did not amount to so much!—by the name of Lena Gilbert, who bought the now-decrepit house because she was a descendant of Lachlan's and wished to restore the property. I was saddened to see its state and remembered it in its former glory. Katrina and I visited Lachlan on several occasions and I considered him a friend—as did General Washington—and she continued to visit after my interment in the cave. But I get ahead of myself.

Lena Gilbert had apparently disappeared shortly after arriving at the house, and Captain Irving contacted Abigail immediately because her representatives sent information to him that included a mention of Katrina's name. We arrived at the house to discover the mutilated body of Lena's bodyguard, and numerous signs of a supernatural presence. Abigail, interestingly, was quite fearful. I had not thought her able to evince timidity, but she confessed to me a deep fright of haunted houses—and such Fredericks Manor clearly was. We immediately observed claw marks on the floor and every door in the house slammed shut, trapping us therein. Abigail saw a ghost and pursued it; I, who could not perceive it, found my way to the library, where my gaze fell upon an edition of *Gulliver's Travels* contemporary with my last visit to Fredericks Manor. It was out of place, displaying none of the dust that had settled over the rest of the house. As one unconsciously does, I riffled the pages and discovered a letter—and not any letter, but one I had written to Katrina; more incredibly, the letter I wrote and left in the care of Samuel Adams, to be delivered to her in the event of my death.

My beloved Katrina,

If you are reading this letter, I have perished at the hands of forces allied with the Crown. There are things you must know. It may be that I have fallen to a musket ball or tomahawk, or the diseases which have ravaged the camps of soldiers since time immemorial. I must be quick, and restrain myself from all but the plain facts, the most pressing of which is this: You may be in danger.

I would say more, but if this letter falls into the wrong hands upon my death, I would not have it yield useful intelligence to our enemies. You have seen them at their worst, with poor Arthur Bernard; I beg you take precautions, lest a similar fate befall you. If you do not believe this a prudent request, I beg you to act as if you do. What harm is a little pretense if it be your husband's last request? One thing only I ask of you:

I have given this letter to Samuel Adams. If it is not he who delivers it into your hands, look to your safety. If it is he, make contact at once with General Washington. He will protect you.

We had too few years together, my love. Many a night I spent in dreary soldiers' camps, dreaming of the life we would have together when the war was over, the colonies free, and we free as well. I dreamed of the children we would have together. I had thought to grow old with you. Now I can only express my sorrow that this dream has been torn from us. I trust we will see each other again, in the afterlife promised to those who believe. I have not always been a devout man, but I believe my soul unstained by evil, and I have tried as best I knew how to do what was right.

I am, and remain, in this world and the next,

Forever yours,

Ichabod

This letter's presence in Fredericks Manor was a mystery. Had Katrina returned here after placing me in the cave? If so, why had she not kept the letter? And how had Lena Gilbert come into possession of it, for surely she was how the copy of the book had come to Fredericks Manor.

Those questions burned in my mind as Abigail and I searched for Lena. I spoke to her of a black woman named Grace Dixon, whom Lachlan had freed and employed—but that term does little justice to her importance in the work of Fredericks Manor. She was its heart and soul, the working hands who made Lachlan's grand ideas into deeds. We located Lena, bound by animated roots in a parlor closet. I cut her free. The roots discharged a foul dark blood, and shortly after a scarecrow, animated by the demonic forces that had taken root—quite literally—inside the house, attacked us. We evaded it while trying to learn more from Lena, who revealed that Katrina had in fact returned to Fredericks Manor after my death, and shortly before the disappearance of Lachlan Fredericks himself. She had heard rumors that Lachlan was a warlock—and I now suspected this as well, though it had of course never occurred to me when I knew him. Moreover, Lena suspected that some magical purpose was behind Katrina's final visit to the house.

Lena and I were separated from Abigail while the three of us dodged the scarecrow, which captured Lena again with the aid of a swarm of crows. Fighting off both scarecrow and crows (who, if I may be permitted a moment of grim humor, were not the least put off by the scarecrow's presence), we located Lena in the house's root cellar, in the grip of the scarecrow, now somehow united with a monstrous mass of fleshy roots and tendrils. Abigail shot into the roots and the scarecrow released Lena, with the roots' dark blood befouling all three of us.

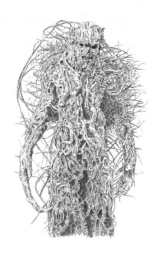

I have been avoiding committing a certain thing to paper but can avoid it no longer.

I have learned that Katrina returned to Fredericks Manor because she was friendless, a fugitive . . . and with child.

My child.

Our child. Our boy.

I am a father.

Not _am_, but _was_. I was a father. There was a child I never knew.

I am at a loss. Would that some wisdom, some consolation, would appear to me and vitiate the unbearable pain of this knowledge. To have had a child and lost him is a sorrow that has broken stronger men than I; to have had a child and never known . . .

Unbearable, yes. All the same, I must bear it. I must.

Can I?

We escaped by virtue of a further apparition of Grace Dixon—for it was she who had appeared to Abigail shortly after our initial entry—pantomiming her assistance in helping Katrina and our newborn son escape Fredericks Manor when this supernatural creature attacked them at the exact moment of my son's birth. Moloch wanted my child—of course! For is that not his nature? Did not all scholars and demonologists take pains to point out his special interest in children? Had I known . . . ! He was thwarted only through the sacrifice of Lachlan Fredericks, who died ensuring that my wife and son could escape. This is a debt I can never repay, save by purging the house of its evil and ensuring that I carry on his work. I did the former, returning to the house after Abigail and Lena were safely outside and cutting the creature to pieces with an axe. I lost my temper and gave myself utterly over to rage—yet I do not regret it. Let Moloch's minions be warned that they threaten those dear to me at peril of their existence.

I slept little last night as I grappled with this new knowledge. Abandoning the quest for sleep well before dawn, I walked from the cabin into the city of Sleepy Hollow and have been reading in the archives. Abigail is here. There is something I must show her.

Abigail is gone to enjoy Thanksgiving dinner with her sister. I begged off, fearing my current state of mind would make me unsuited to the occasion. But before she left, we opened a package from Lena that arrived last night.

It seems she has traced the history of Fredericks Manor with some diligence, and uncovered a trove of information about that notable house's residents and their descendants. Among those descendants: one Abigail Mills, daughter of Lori Roberts and the several-times great-granddaughter of Grace Dixon. My instinct was correct: We are bound together, we Two Witnesses, by ancient ties. Grace Dixon delivered my son into this world, and shepherded him to safety from Moloch's minions; and now, after two centuries, the descendant of Grace Dixon is my irreplaceable ally in the next phase of the war to contain Moloch and prevent him from unleashing the Horsemen of the Apocalypse. Again I am staggered by the clockwork nature of it all; wherever one might assume coincidence, there instead one finds plans laid in the eighteenth century and now in the twenty-first beginning to hatch.

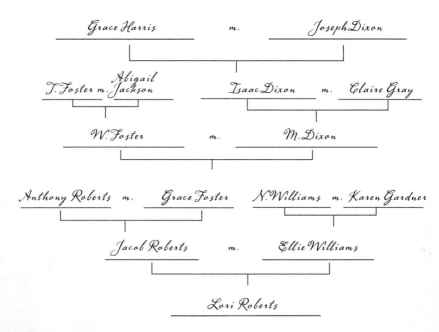

Abigail is struggling with the knowledge of her own entanglement in the events of the centuries-long war between dark and light here in Sleepy Hollow. I believe she is also agonized by the realization that she is granted visions of her ancestors, recalling as this does the traumatic moment when she spied Moloch as a child. Her cold, reasoning approach to life is threatened, and I fear she will address the threat in some untoward way. Such a division must naturally be unhealthy for the mind. I will speak to her of this, perhaps, if I can hit upon a conversational gambit that will not seem patronizing to her.

Also unhealthy for the mind: knowing one has had a son, but not knowing what has become of him. My son two hundred years, perhaps, in his own grave. Do I live among his descendants? I should like to examine the Internet for persons surnamed Crane in this area. I should like to see each of them, regard them, discern if possible any trace of myself therein . . . perhaps then I would feel reconciled to this second life.

What manner of man did he become? Had he a happy life? Were there children? Am I even now surrounded by my own descendants? What do they know of me, if they know aught?

It occurs to me that a search for Crane might well prove fruitless because my son might have lived his life under another name. Katrina left this world scarcely a year after my own departure, did she not? The boy would have been adopted. What became of my son? Who raised him? Did they know of his true parentage, and if so, did they tell him?

Wrenched out of time, I am wrenched from all I loved—and wrenched as well from those to whom I owed love. For the creation of a child is a mighty debt, and may only be repaid through the correct raising of a child in love and guidance. That I was unable to do. That I will never be able to do.

What was his name?

I can write of my son no more. For what does one say? I know not what sort of man he grew up to be, nor what other unholy plans Moloch hatched to ensnare him. . . .

And why did Katrina not tell me she was with child? Why not in 1781? Why not now, when we have spoken in my dreams?

I must not let my mind spiral inward, gnawing on questions without answers. Instead I will seek those answers. Chief among them is the question of what became of my son; but hard on the heels of that is the dark suspicion that Moloch keeps me alive because he wishes me to procreate once more—perhaps only that he may have the pleasure of taking from me another child, as my long sleep deprived me of knowing my first.

Shake it off, Ichabod. That is what they say in this time. Shake it off.

I will read a little more and then hope to find a ride back to the cabin. If none is available, the walk will suit me. I have enjoyed walking since I was a boy, and it is easy to lose the habit and the enjoyment of it in this age when the keys to an automobile seemingly jingle in every pocket.

———————

It approaches midnight, and the grand armies of Black Friday mobilize—but elsewhere, as I am ensconced at Trout Lake, far from the temples of commerce. I spent this Thanksgiving Day endeavoring to be thankful, and largely failing.

A last note as Black Friday commences, and the bells of getting and spending toll throughout the land—although only in the Eastern time zone. I have learned recently that America's vastness has demanded the creation of different times for different areas, and indeed that this happens across the world, so at this moment it is five o'clock in the morning in Britain. How odd—yet how perfectly sensible, since the rotation of the Earth brings light and dark at such a predictable pace. But I digress, the note . . .

I have seen soldiers' scrip. I have seen currencies and coin issued by Britain, France, and each of the colonies. I have bought goods with pounds and shillings, Spanish cobs, Continental dollars, Virginia ha'pennies, Rhode Island ship tokens, wampum, beaver skins . . . but never a rectangle of plastic with a strip of magnetically encoded information on one side. Is this even money? One can slide these plastic rectangles through machines crafted for the purpose. These machines speak directly to the bank holding the purchaser's money, and deduct the amount in question. Surely these computers possess some intelligence; otherwise how would such a thing be possible? A "cashless economy" is spoken of; but how can any man trust a machine to keep his money? I certainly would not. The only real money is that in a pocket. All else is numbers only, an endless series of promissory notes. Abigail, of course, finds this quite funny. Quoth she: "You're the youngest curmudgeon I ever met, Crane."

I gather some of the coins in my pocket are quite valuable to collectors now. Should I ever have need of extra resources, I shall not hesitate to part with them!—although I would not be able to spend them on the new sibling of Black Friday, the Cyber Monday. On this day The Amazon holds unchallenged sway, and millions of dollars vanish invisibly over the Internet, as the post grows heavy with the cargo of packages traveling from storehouses all over the country to houses, occupied by people who no longer even wish to leave their homes for purposes of commerce. How strange and isolating the apotheosis of convenience can turn out to be.

I have now seen two of the popular sporting pastimes of this nation, and I find the differences between them instructive.

Baseball is quite pastoral, and its complexities soon become apparent to the patient observer. Even in the amateur form in which I first encountered it, the charm of the game was clear: the imperative to round the bases and return home, each completed circle advancing a team toward victory. Baseball is a game of circles, of cycles, and of eternal things. A circle has no end, and the territory of the home run encompasses the infinite distance beyond the fence. I have since watched more baseball on television, and am utterly charmed by it. There was a game known as stoolball in the Britain of my youth, as well as cricket, and both seem clearly to be predecessors of baseball, though I am no scholar of sport.

Football is quite different. All is measured to the inch and no man may step beyond the boundaries of the field lest play stop immediately. The field is a rectangle, rigorously measured, unlike the stadia of baseball, which vary considerably in dimension and aspect. A joyless game, I find, and even so, it is the unifying force of Thanksgiving, even more than the ritualized consumption of a turkey that bears as much resemblance to the wild bird as I do to a grizzly bear. It is quite a martial exercise, and television announcers emphasize that impression by the constant invocation of the lexicon of battle. Never, outside the halls of governmental deliberation, have I seen an event in which so much is said about so little.

And what in the name of all that is holy have dancing girls in quite scandalous décolleté to do with a sporting event? It makes one yearn for baseball—or for the football I remember from England, in which players used their feet for more than running. This game is apparently known as soccer now, and is perplexingly unpopular in the United States despite its adoration in virtually all other nations.

Purgatory. One must trace the concept back to its roots. It is primarily a conceit of the Roman Catholics now, but the idea reaches back much farther than the history of the Roman church, into the ancient traditions of the Hebrews. They prayed over their dead to purify the souls of the departed and ease their passage into the afterlife. The Egyptians, in their polytheistic way, also believed in a measuring of the soul after death, which had the result of permitting passage to the afterlife—or of annihilation by an underworld monster that stood waiting in Osiris's Hall of Judgment. Christianity took this belief and imposed a more rigorous conception, positing Purgatory not as a place where the recently dead were judged but as a place that is no place, where souls spent time in a process of purification until they achieved worthiness to ascend into the Kingdom of Heaven.

From Katrina I have learned that the truth is somewhat more complex. Moloch watches over Purgatory and snatches unworthy souls to be his minions. Others he cannot touch but is permitted to hold for a certain period of time. Still others he can only observe as they pass through. But in no account have I read of Purgatory being a forest; it puts me in mind of the early Puritans, writing of the trackless New World wilderness as the abode of the devil, waiting to be tamed and civilized by axe and plow and Scripture. Is this wilderness beyond the mirror an American Purgatory, then, derived from the character of those most devout of America's first colonists? Doubtless I shall never know, but in any event Katrina appears to be a particular case. The nature of Moloch's hold on

Things to remember:
- turn off lights by pressing switch
- water in the shower gets really hot and really cold and will run out
- the big box in the kitchen keeps food cold and it will last longer than a day
- images on the tele-vision? might be real
- taxes are really high
- coffee shops are everywhere
- electricity was put into service in early 1900s—Lt. Mills says it is a good thing
- skinny jeans are terrible
- find a tailor (?)
- learn the rules of baseball

her is unclear to me. I understand why he wants her—to dangle as a reward for Van Brunt's continued loyalty—but I do not understand what rule of Purgatory makes it possible for him to keep her there. Perhaps it has to do with her practice of witchcraft; perhaps it is due to the magic she worked to prevent my death from the wound inflicted by Abraham Van Brunt; perhaps he is transgressing against the laws of heaven in holding her, and it is part of the demonic war he wages to bring about the Apocalypse and the End of Days.

There is only one way to find out.

How dispassionately I write, when my heart and mind churn with rage and anxiety.

I will reach Katrina. I must and shall, and have already taken the first steps to make it possible. Abigail will likely not approve, but it will not be she who undertakes the risk. It is not she who suffers the knowledge of her beloved under Moloch's fearful sway.

———

All this sitting and writing makes me mad. Winter is coming. I should lay in a supply of wood. The feel of an axe handle in my hands will be a welcome change from this pen.

One had little leisure while fighting for the colonies' independence, but little is a far cry from none at all. Some of the officers in the rebel army possessed chessboards. The campfires, as campfires no doubt have been for millennia, were gathering places for ribald stories and comradely conversation.

For diversion beyond this, there was little. I regarded the stars, and where I knew no constellations I invented them.

Contrast that with my current state. One can only spend so much time staring at the walls of a cabin belonging to a dead man. And extraordinary as the Mills sisters are, their camaraderie is

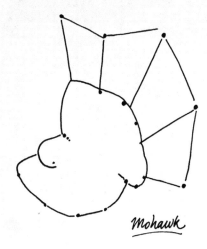

Mohawk

sharpshooter

⌐ nb: this is pretty much
an upside-down version
of Hercules

Naked Bear

Regulus

Draco, but looks
kind of like the
Eastern USA

neither as bawdy nor as simple as it was among my revolutionary brothers. Still, Abigail and I have watched a movie together, which is what people of this time watch instead of the theater. Her television is quite enormous, much larger than Sheriff Corbin's, with a corresponding increase in volume from "surround sound," which true devotees regard as indispensable to the movie experience. Astonishing! It was pell-mell noise, full of what they call "special effects," which from what I gather is a necessary part of all movies. It appears to be some sort of imperative to make things explode whenever possible—as if every story were in fact a fireworks display. I could understand practically nothing of what was said; the actors made the most absurd faces, excelling even the garish style of performance of Sheridan or Wycherley on the stages of London. The entire spectacle struck me as marvelous but nonsensical. Abigail laughed uproariously when I told her this. "That's our age, all right," she said. "Marvelous and nonsensical."

With the echoes of that movie still in my mind, I have been thinking I would very much love to play a game of chess. Perhaps Henry Parish plays; he seems the kind of man who would. In other circumstances I would seek friendship with him, and if we all remain alive after the Horsemen are routed and Moloch defeated, one of the first things I will do is set up a chessboard and offer Henry Parish the white pieces. A different sort of camaraderie than a soldiers' bonfire, to be sure—yet one to which I am much more suited.

———————

Another thought, belatedly provoked by the viewing of football, many of whose players shave their heads. This is not a practice solely of sportsmen, either. A great many of the men I see have hair no longer than an eyelash. This was an unusual choice both in the American colonies and in England. Men shaved their heads then to avoid the infestation of lice, or if their profession or station required the daily wearing of a wig. A shaved head was also a punishment for certain crimes, designed to humiliate and stigmatize the person in question. I have been fortunate to avoid the ubiquitous plague of lice, a blessing I attribute to a combination of luck, Providence, and my instinct toward fastidiousness.

I have never considered cutting my own hair, save to prevent it from growing long enough to interfere with the natural motions and use of my hands, or on those occasions when formality has demanded I don a powdered wig—which I detest. Few those instances have been, and for their rarity I am fervently thankful.

It seems, in any event, that the stigma of the shaved head has long since died out. For my part, I will keep my hair as it is. Not for me the luxuries of the hair salon.

It seems the Sisterhood of the Radiant Heart were not the pure allies I had understood them to be. It was they Katrina fled after she stopped my soul on the verge of fleeing my mortal remains and placed me in the cave until I could be revived. She went as far as Europe, and there discovered she was with child. As a widow with child on the run from both the British, who would hang her for a spy, and her coven, who would destroy her as a turncoat for the sorcery she worked to keep me alive, she had no choice but to go to Fredericks Manor.

I learned this from Katrina by having Henry Parish strangle me to the point of death, thereby easing my path to Purgatory. Katrina was startled to see me there, and I was decidedly more than surprised to see that we were in the hallowed environs of Trinity Church—yet in Purgatory. The illusions of demons are without limit. She was lighting a votive, and had many questions to ask me, but knowing I had but little time, I insisted my own queries must take precedence. Too, I was battling conflicting impulses. I wanted to sweep her into my arms and remain with her forever; I wanted to interrogate her, chastise her, demand her reasons for never telling me of our son. There was no time to work through such turmoil, so I remained focused on what I needed to learn.

Our son's name was Jeremy, after my grandfather. She was forced to surrender the baby boy to the care of Grace Dixon, fearing what would happen to him if the witches of her coven found her before she had made arrangements for his rearing. She was hunted by the Four-Who-Speak-as-One, a quartet of powerful witches of the Radiant Heart, whose combined might she could not hope to oppose.

We would have spoken more, but the entire edifice of the church began to shudder, as if under the assault of a being of monstrous strength. I caught a glimpse of it as I receded from Purgatory back into the world, where Abigail and Henry Parish awaited my tale with considerable impatience. Upon hearing what had transpired in Purgatory, Parish made ready to leave, but Abigail prevailed upon him to stay a while longer and assist us in our quest to understand what had happened to Jeremy—and what we might do to release Katrina from Purgatory. Our first stop was the historical society library, where we navigated first the librarian's strong desire to be left alone with her books and then the cryptic organization of her stacks. Shortly we discovered that Grace and her husband died in a fire, and Jeremy had survived; but this news was soon more than counterbalanced by the discovery that Jeremy was said by the townspeople of the time to be able to start fires when his emotions overmastered him. Immediately I suspected that he must have inherited his mother's native talent for witchcraft—and, in addition, I found myself in the delicate position of expressing remorse for my child's role in the deaths of Abigail's ancestors. She, hardheaded and stoic as always, dismissed the idea of blaming the boy, and we had no chance to speak of it further, for a scream from the parking lot drew us outside . . . where we found the librarian, Isobel Hudson, savagely murdered.

Sometimes it seems as if everyone I speak to in Sleepy Hollow is immediately in danger of his or her life. Soon all but the suicidal and deranged will avoid me like the plague.

[December 24]

We transferred some of the society's materials back to the archives. Henry noted the presence of the sign of the Sisterhood of the Radiant Heart on a golden box—Isobel Hudson had been one of them! Henry, whose senses are attuned to stimuli far subtler than those more normal humans can apprehend—for how else is a Sin Eater to detect and consume and purge sins?—recoiled from the box, saying it smelled of dire things: anger, fear, death . . .

Inside it was a drawing my son had done as a boy. The paper was frail and cracking, but I could almost see his hand holding the charcoal, the other keeping the paper flat, tiny fingers spread . . . Abigail had seen the doll represented on the paper in the vision granted by Grace Dixon. Katrina had given him that doll, she explained—then Henry happened to touch the drawing. His eyes turned black as the void, and he recounted the tale of Jeremy's suffering in a Puritan orphanage, where in 1794—at the age of twelve—he was beaten by a clergyman and bled on the doll. His powers, channeled through the blood and fueled by the rage, transformed the doll into a fearsome creature driven by the imperative to protect him.

That same creature had followed me back out of Purgatory—for I realized it was the creature I had seen a moment before I was returned to this world. The creature was loose in this time, and it was hunting down those whom it deemed a threat to Jeremy—though Jeremy himself was no longer alive to protect. Where, then, would it next strike?

I could not make all the pieces of the puzzle fit together—Henry, however, could. He noted the presence of carnival ticket stubs dating back one hundred years in Isobel Hudson's safe, and he said something that suddenly caused me to see everything in a different light: "Jeremy is molded from your clay."

Clay.

I went to General Washington's Bible, hearing the echo of Katrina's voice telling me answers to future challenges would be found therein—and also hearing Henry Parish, earlier today, explain that puzzles operated by obscuring the key to their solution rather than the solution itself. Clay . . . a creature created to protect . . .

It is a golem. It must be.

Further, in Isobel Hudson's possessions Abigail found a flyer for a carnival act: a quartet of seers billed as the Four-Who-Speak-as-One: Sisters of Spirit and Clairvoyance.

It has taken too long, but at last we know what is happening. The witches who banished both Katrina and the golem are hiding in plain sight, as carnival fortune-tellers. The golem will find them, and soon.

It appears we are going to the carnival—and to save the four witches, the Four-Who-Speak-as-One, the very four responsible for banishing my Katrina to Purgatory. I would willingly see them perish at the hands of the golem, but I must master those darker impulses—for if they banished Katrina, it is they who can recall

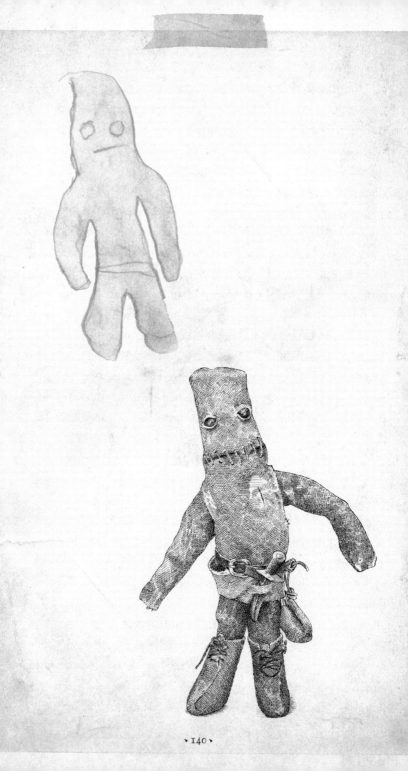

her. Henry Parish is in agreement with this, and we also agree that Moloch would be weakened by a free Katrina, for then he would have no sway over the Horseman. And so we must fight the golem that protected my son, to prevent it from ending the lives of the witches who killed my son.

Being a warrior for heaven is a difficult path.

The lore of the golem most famously rests on the story of the Golem of Prague, that mighty defender of that city's Jews in their ghetto. That golem was created from clay, by the inscription of the Hebrew word אמת—emet, meaning "truth." It was destroyed by wiping away the first letter, turning emet into מת, met—meaning "dead." The Golem of Prague, like Jeremy's golem, eventually had to be destroyed because it was too violent in defense of its masters.

Four-Who-Speak-as-One. Is the secret in their names?

Isa Mal Nahum Jer

Jer Isa Nahum Mal

Malisa Jerisa Nahummal Jermal Maljerisa Jermalisa Jernahum

Perhaps they must be scrambled. Anagrams are linguistic witchery. The alchemy of letters and syllables.

Nahum = an anagram of HUMAN

Mal = Latin prefix meaning "bad"

Jer = ?

Isa = ?

The key to understanding a language puzzle—in addition to Henry's insight that understanding a puzzle's method is more crucial than grinding through the individual clues—lies in the relative frequencies of the letters, as with ciphers. Is this a cipher of some sort?

Mal-Nahum = bad human?

Jermal and Jerisa = unknown in any language with which I am familiar

Malisa =

Isamal =

Maljer =

I am doodling. This is a waste of time. Use your brain. I have it!

Nahum, of course, was a prophet. This was so evident I failed to see it as germane, suspecting there must be a deeper puzzle. His name means "comforter," which seems an odd moniker for a prophet; their writings seldom comfort any but those who desire the End Times. He wrote with quite remarkable vividness of the destruction of Nineveh, which he believed would occur as a consequence of Assyria's heresies and oppression of the Jews.

Isa = Isaiah. "God is salvation." The greatest of Hebrew prophets, the leading prophetic voice of Judah during the ruling years of four kings: Uzziah, Jotham, Ahaz, and Hezekiah. He too lived in the shadow of Assyrian bellicosity. From Isaiah 37: "Whom hast thou reproached and blasphemed? And against whom hast thou exalted thy voice, and lifted up thine eyes on high? Even against the Holy One of Israel." How tempting to read this as a prophecy of the demonic war—and perhaps the witches of the Radiant Heart saw it thus?

Jer = Jeremiah. "God exalts." Known as the Weeping Prophet for the keening of his laments. He was unrelenting in his attacks on the sins of the people of Judah; they in return beat and abused him throughout his life, throwing him at least once into a cistern and plotting against his life. The Babylonian king Nebuchadnezzar treated him with honor when he conquered Judah—a conquest Jeremiah had predicted, and blamed on the sinful predilections of Judaeans. He, more than the other Hebrew prophets, demanded that every soul confront its individual relationship with the Almighty, and rely not on widely held opinions to guide it.

Mal = Malachi. "Messenger." An unusual name speculated to be a pseudonym, for *messenger* is also the word the Hebrew Bible uses to refer to the beings we have now come to call angels. The book that bears his name is fervently messianic, and beloved of those who wish to find in the late Hebrew prophets evidence that they wrote of the coming of Christ.

Prophets all. (And, one notes, male prophets.) The Four-Who-Speak-as-One took the names of male prophets from the later books of the Jewish Bible.

What can this mean?

Henry Parish has finally gotten on his train back to the city. I trust the delay was worthwhile, providing as it did the spectacle of the golem wrecking the grounds of the carnival after the Four-Who-Speak-as-One met me and matter-of-factly acknowledged that their deaths had arrived with me. I had no intent to kill *them*—quite the opposite—but they would not be dissuaded.

And they were right. But before they died, I learned more about my son's life . . . and death. For it was they who killed him. They had a reason, so they said. The golem had begun killing too many denizens of Sleepy Hollow, wherever it perceived a threat to

Jeremy. The Four-Who-Speak-as-One found him, and worked a charm to imprison the golem in Purgatory. Then they offered Jeremy the protection of their coven, since they coveted his power—but also, I believe, because they felt a lingering sense of guilt over their hounding of Katrina.

He refused; whether from fear or mistrust they did not say and I will never know.

Fearing to leave him unleashed, with too much power and not enough restraint, the Four-Who-Speak-as-One worked a charm together and stopped his heart. They did not flinch from the admission, even knowing that the golem was coming to render the only justice it knew.

I let it. I made no attempt to save them. I faced the golem willingly to preserve the lives of my friends, but the witches who murdered my son? I, who had come to save them from the golem, lifted no finger when the golem rampaged into their tent and ended them. I will, for the rest of the days granted to me, feel a small twinge of regret . . . but as with my other transgressions, I will learn to make a place for that guilt within my soul, and answer for it when I must. I have never hated any human as I hated those four.

It was Henry's insight—he, who sees through to the heart of puzzles—that if the golem was created by Jeremy's blood, it must be destroyed by his blood. Half of his blood is my blood. Of course Henry had this small epiphany when viewing my blood on a shard of mirror, so we must not anoint him with the oil of omniscience quite yet.

I spoke to the golem. I tried to make it understand that its commission was no longer active, that the boy it existed to protect was no more, but in the end it could not reason and I was forced to destroy it. Doing so was far more difficult for me than the act of killing the men I have killed; it was the last link with my son, the only other being charged with his care after the death of his mother. When it was gone, all that remained was the doll. I will keep it. It is the last thing on earth my son touched.

Before Henry Parish left, he told me something which I found immensely heartening. He understood now, he said—in his characteristically understated manner—that it was indeed his duty to render the assistance of his particular abilities to the Witnesses' battle against evil. We also spoke, while we were in the tunnels, of his parents' deaths, and the bond between father and son (thinking of which weighs heavily on my mind these days). A sensitive man, Henry Parish, and not just because he is a Sin Eater. He is a good man, who has suffered much and not let his suffering twist or destroy him. I am very glad to count him as an ally.

After he left for the train station, Abigail gave me a Christmas stocking. I am charmed. Perhaps I am not entirely immune to holiday cheer after all!

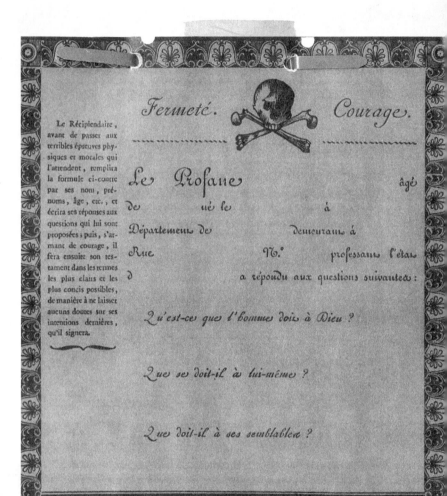

Fermeté.   *Courage.*

Le Récipiendaire, avant de passer aux terribles épreuves physiques et morales qui l'attendent, remplira la formule ci-contre par ses nom, prénoms, âge, etc., et écrira ses réponses aux questions qui lui sont proposées ; puis, s'armant de courage, il fera ensuite son testament dans les termes les plus clairs et les plus concis possibles, de manière à ne laisser aucuns doutes sur ses intentions dernières, qu'il signera.

Le Profane   âgé de   né le   à

Département de   demeurant à

Rue   N.°   professant l'état

d   a répondu aux questions suivantes :

Qu'est-ce que l'homme doit à Dieu ?

Que se doit-il à lui-même ?

Que doit-il à ses semblables ?

TESTAMENT.

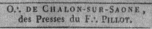

O∴ DE CHALON-SUR-SAONE,
des Presses du F∴ PILLOT.

Jeremy. I write to you though I am the only one who will ever read the words. I am sorry, my son. I am sorry I did not survive to see your birth. I am sorry I could not save you from the brutality of the orphanage, or from the elemental urges that overwhelmed you as a boy. I am sorry I was not there to raise you properly. I am sorry for the sorrows of your life, the fear that led you to turn to the golem. I hope it was a friend to you, and not solely a mindless guardian. I am sorry the Sisterhood of the Radiant Heart could not persuade you to join them, and that they could not respect your refusal.

My own father was a difficult man, disapproving of my choice to become a soldier and adamantly opposed to my allegiance with the Continentals. I swore to myself when your mother and I were married that I would not be so hard and inflexible with my own son—yet I never had the chance to better his example. Believe me, my son, I would have, if granted the opportunity to see your birth and infancy. That is the worst failure of a man: absence when his children need him. For that, too, I am sorry.

When the good men and women of the world do such things as this, what is it we fight for? Would Moloch be worse? He consumed children in fire, and the Radiant Heart reached out and stopped your radiant heart, ending your life, which veered from confusion to tragedy. How am I to live with this? How do I maintain faith?

That is the question. It has no answer, save to take the example of Job and know that perseverance is its own reward. If no man ever kept to the path of righteousness despite the cruelties of the world and of heaven, all hope would be lost. Right action matters. But it is hard to go on.

This, this is the doubt without which there cannot be faith. But

I would have a little less of one, and I would have the other come a little more easily. Moloch taunts me, for he knows my faith has feet of clay. But yet I will be strong.

At least I have this doll that you touched. It protected you for a time—as I could not.

Moloch has changed his tack. He must believe the wind to be shifting against him. He drew me into the Mirror World—Purgatory—but only for a moment. "When you know the saint's name, War will take form." This was Moloch's riddle. He added a threat, that he would have Abigail's soul and I would be the one to deliver it to him.

He is angry now. He drew me to Purgatory, but he could not hold me. Instead he sought to cow me. I take that as a sign of fear.

And just like that, my crisis of faith is over.

Before I forget, Captain Irving reports unusual occurrences during his most recent visit to his daughter on the island of Manhattan. He suspects an evil influence is following him, and is possibly a threat to his daughter, Macey. Poor creature, she is confined to a wheelchair. A spitfire personality, nonetheless.

[January 3]

Abigail has brought me clothing. We were to go shopping together, but at the last moment I demurred, unable to face the throngs at the immense marketplace known as a "shopping mall." I require solace, being of a scholarly nature and more suited, I fear, to the company of books than of my fellow humans. She is regarding me now with ill-disguised impatience as I scribble this down rather than greeting her and rousing myself to try the fit of the clothing she has purchased.

I will be frank. I despise the fashions of this age. I look around me and it seems that in 2013, one may dress according to one's whims. Suits of clothes are side by side with shirts bearing hideous slogans and designs. Short pants are common among adults, which is an innovation I might have found quite welcome in the sweltering climes of Georgia—yet it seems quite out of place here in New York, where the temperatures are cool enough to make short pants seem immodest.

Even trousers are worn in various ways: cinched at the hips by a belt, hitched up to the waist, even left to sag down to mid-buttock; incredibly these last attract no attention from police despite their flagrant transgression against common decency. The dress of women is form-fitting to a degree that would have paralyzed any man of the eighteenth century, and I will say no more lest that track of thought lead me to impure thoughts. Also, I despise zippers.

The fault, however, is not in the fashions, for they have faded throughout the ages, and no particular moment is responsible for the foolishness of its dress; no, the fault lies in me, for I have come to clutch at my difference as an act of self-preservation. My clothing, which survived battles and army encampments—not to mention two centuries and more lying in a cave—has become dear to me. I have always resisted imbuing physical objects with emotional significance; however the impulse is nigh impossible to resist when all that ties me to my former life is my clothing. I am, it seems, not quite prepared to admit that I live in this future—though to deny it of course is rank idiocy.

Abigail has begun to tap her foot. That is a signal whose meaning has survived the centuries. I must put down my pen and adorn myself with the raiment of 2013. Trepidation, thy name is new clothing.

———————

These damnable clothes. How did I let Abigail beguile me into changing from the dress that suits me into these outlandish garments? I can scarcely move. Tight-fitting breeches were the style in 1781, and apparently again in this time—but this denim fabric clutches at me in a way that wool never did. Perhaps I shall grow accustomed to it, or perhaps I will stake out the territory of the unfashionable for myself; I am no fop, and never was.

———————

I have heard of very few instances in which a demon could migrate at will from one body to another. Demonic possession typically is ended in one of two ways. Either the demon abandons its host or it is exorcised. While thinking of the Devil's Trap some days ago, I copied down an exorcism ritual. There are a number of them, each with its own partisans and its own efficacies in certain situations. Here is one I saw copied into a document once folded into General Washington's Bible.

> Exorcizamus te, omnis immundus spiritus, omnis satanica potestas, omnis incursio infernalis adversarii, omnis legio, et secta diabolica,
> Ergo draco maledicte et sectio
> Ergo draco maledicte et legio secta diabolica
> Ut Ecclésiam tuam secúra tibi fácias servire libertáte, te rogámus, audi nos.

And while we have come to rest on the topic of Washington's Bible, I believe I shall be forced to remove it from my preferred location, inside one of Sheriff Corbin's heavy locking file cabinets. Captain Irving came to the archive and spoke to us of a demon he suspects is in Sleepy Hollow, flitting from person to person and leaving each of its former hosts with no memory of its possession. He previously saw it in Manhattan, where it threatened his daughter ... and now it apparently has designs on Washington's Bible. I am reading through it again, studying the profuse marginalia. Its pages give off the faint but unmistakable odor of rot.

Abigail has located a thick sheaf of records and documents related to possession. Sheriff Corbin's research interests were both broad and deep. I should have very much liked to have met him. Among these documents on possession is a dossier recounting his apprehension of a woman taken over by a demon with the ability to leap from body to body, leaving each previous vessel with no memory of what had transpired during his or her possession. We studied this record and located a videocassette of Corbin's interview with the young woman in question. On the video, Corbin gave particulars of the case and then turned the camera on the subject of the possession, who was none other than Jennifer Mills.

PROPERTY OF SLEEPY HOLLOW SHERIFF DEPARTMENT

POSSESSION

Oldest known references come from Sumer. Very rarely attested in the Old Testament; much more frequent in Gospels and Acts. Jesus casts out demons, is accused of being possessed. Why so much more common? Unknown. Known in most cultures and religions—Koran, Surah al-Baqarah 2:275.

Typical symptoms: Increased strength. Rage and aversion to symbols holy to the local culture. Knowledge of things the person could not know—including languages—sometimes speaking in tongues.

Most shamanic cultures have rituals in place to expel demons. Physical intervention also common. Some of the earliest medical procedures known to history were performed to exorcise a spirit. Trepanation, drilling holes in the skull to release pressure, was common for centuries—believed to create a way for demons to escape. Another practice: Force nauseating drinks on the possessed, to disgust the demon. In some cultures people who survived dangerous illness changed their names, so the demon that caused the illness wouldn't be able to find them again. Variation: some cultures call sick or possessed people by ugly or hateful names to force the demon to leave. Then the person's true name is used again.

Often, exorcised demons are sent back to the plane/dimension/realm of their origin. At times they are destroyed. On rare occasions it's attested that they were imprisoned in another form—most famously with Jesus and the pigs, Matthew 8, Mark 5, Luke 8.

Religious hucksters typically claim that addicts, mentally ill people, etc., are possessed by demons. I've seen real demonic possession and it's got nothing to do with your other personal problems. If a demon rides you, it's because that demon wants you. Example: Wendigo curse.

Sage, cedar, camphor, other herbs commonly make up part of exorcism rituals. Also, salt. Demons can be expelled sometimes by forcing the possessed person to drink salt water: both nauseating and anti-demon because of the salt itself.

SNEEZING. Often held to be a sign of possession, or that demons are near. Not sure if there's anything to it, otherwise you'd have to believe there are a lot of demons around during allergy season. (Allergies as demonic possession? People with bad hay fever probably believe it.)

YAWNING. Also said to be a sign that demons are near, and forcing the mouth open to enter. Various practices have developed to fight this—some Hindus crack their knuckles after yawning to frighten away the encroaching spirit.

~

Recent CASE: V. rare to see demons transferring bodies but I've observed it with this young woman. Have been unable to make an exorcism stick—also have no idea where the demon goes when it is not riding her. The subject has no memory of possession between incidents but is aware they are happening. Tough kid. See attached video recording. Possible to perform an exorcism over a wide area, to force demon to abandon body-jumping? Unknown. More research required. She needs help and I'm not sure I can give it to her.

What a harrowing experience possession must be. I pray I never experience it. Miss Jenny refused at first to view the tape, although she knew of the incident; she had no memory of her possession—as Corbin stated in the file—and she had no desire to be reminded of it. Abigail convinced her only by confronting her with the potential danger to Captain Irving's Macey—Miss Jenny has a soft spot, as the saying goes, for the young girl. I believe she sees some of her own strength of will in Macey, as do I.

She consented, and we viewed the next portion of the tape, wherein the demon possessing Jennifer spoke of the Horseman. It warned Corbin he would die by the Horseman's hand—which was true—and that the Horseman would also kill Abigail. Then she suffered some sort of violent episode and the tape broke off, presumably because she damaged the recording equipment.

Watching with us in the archives, Jennifer withdrew into the stony silence that is her primary defense against unwanted facts. She refused to help; she could not help. Clearly she suffered from a deep sense of violation. She left, and we—Abigail, Irving, and I—considered what to do next. Irving left with his family for a safe house, where he was to meet a Father Boland, who had some experience with battling and exorcising demons. It was him Irving had gone to Manhattan to see a few days before.

I caught up with Jennifer before she could drive away and begged her to reconsider. Macey's life was at stake, and perhaps the lives of others as well. Jennifer opened to me, ever so slightly, and admitted—in strictest confidence—that she had been subject to periodic episodes of possession ever since she and Abigail encountered Moloch in the forest when they were young girls. This revelation would have been disturbing enough, but Jennifer added to it a heartbreaking tale of self-sacrifice: The reason for her multiple incarcerations was her unshakable resolve to prevent the de-

Demon

A **demon** or '**daemon**' is a paranormal, often malevolent being prevalent in <u>religion</u>, <u>occultism</u>, <u>literature</u>, fiction, and <u>folklore</u>. The original Greek word <u>*daimon*</u> does not carry the negative connotation initially understood by implementation of the <u>Koine</u> δαιμόνιον (daimonion),[1] and later ascribed to any cognate words sharing the root.

In <u>Ancient Near Eastern religions</u> as well as in the <u>Abrahamic traditions</u>, including ancient and medieval <u>Christian demonology</u>, a demon is considered an <u>unclean spirit</u>, sometimes a <u>fallen angel</u>, the spirit of a deceased human, or a spirit of unknown type which may cause <u>demonic possession</u>, calling for an <u>exorcism</u>. In Western <u>occultism</u> and <u>Renaissance magic</u>, which grew out of an amalgamation of <u>Greco-Roman magic</u>, Jewish demonology, and Christian tradition,[2] a demon is a spiritual entity that may be <u>conjured</u> and controlled.

St. Anthony, the 1480s.

The A[...] a spirit or divine power, much like the <u>Latin</u> *genius* or <u>nur</u>[...] [Gre]ek verb *daiesthai* (to divide, distribute).[3] The Greek conc[...] [w]orks of <u>Plato</u>, where it describes the divine insp[...] [classi]cal Greek concept from its later <u>Christian</u> inte[...] [... fo]r *daemon* or *daimon* rather than *demon*.

Th[...] [notio]ns of evil or malevolence. In fact, εὐδαιμονία eu[...] [... hap]piness. The term first acquired its negative c[...] [... in] the <u>Hebrew Bible</u>, which drew on the mythology of a[...] [inhe]rited by the Koine text of the <u>New Testament</u>. The [... concep]tion of a *demon* (see the Medieval <u>grimoire</u> called the *Ars* [...] [...]t popular culture of Late (Roman) Antiquity. The [... in]clude many Semitic and Near Eastern gods as evaluated

[...] important concept in many modern religions and occultist [... p]opular <u>superstition</u>, largely due to their alleged power to [... temp]orary Western occultist tradition (perhaps epitomized by the [... su]ch as <u>Choronzon</u>, the Demon of the Abyss) is a useful [... psychologi]cal processes (inner demons), though some may also regard it [... so]me scholars[4] believe that large portions of the <u>demonology</u> [... influe]nce on <u>Christianity</u> and <u>Islam</u>, originated from a later form of [...] to Judaism during the Persian era.

<u>Zoroastria</u>[...]

(Newspaper clipping overlay:)

Devil-Casting Rites Cure Boy

Jesuit Priest Routs Evil Spirit

WASHINGTON, Aug. 20 (UPI)— A Jesuit priest using ancient devil-casting rites of the Catholic church has freed a 14-year-old boy of an evil spirit after science failed to "cure" him, church spokesmen said today.

The successful exorcism was reported by the National Catholic Welfare Conference News Service. The service supplied no names or details except to say that the lad was treated without results by medical institutions before the exorcism ritual was invoked.

From other sources it was learned that the lad is the same "haunted boy" whose troubles were reported recently to the Washington Society of Parapsychology. A poltergeist by definition is a mischievous spirit. Parapsychologists are students of manifestations, including psychic phenomena, not covered by more conventional branches of psychological science.

BELPHEGOR
Demon of Discoveries

BELZEBUTH
Prince of Demons, Lord of the Flies

BERITH
Great Duke of Hell

BUER
Great President of Hell

CAACRINOLAAS
High President of Hell

CAYM
High President of Hell

CERBERE
Marquis of Hell

DEUMUS

EURYNOME
Prince of Death

FLAGA

FLAUROS
Grand General of Hell

FORCAS
High President of Hell

FURFUR

GAAP
High President and High Prince of Hell

GOMORY
Duke of Hell

HARBORYM
Duke of Hell

mons riding her from harming her sister. She caused herself to be imprisoned, over and over, to increase the probability that her possessions would occur while she was secured and away from Abigail.

Moved by this tale, I asked Jennifer yet again to aid us. We had learned all we could from Corbin's files; only Jennifer herself could make us see what we were missing. She agreed to another viewing of the tape, and as I write we are playing it over and over, looking for the clue that must be there.

———————

She found it! There was a passage in the recording where Jennifer falls into glossolalia—speaking in tongues—but we had an instinct that there might be a message in this apparent gibberish. By re-recording it and playing it backward—that most fundamental of codes, the reversal—the gibberish was revealed (due to my facility with languages) to be Aramaic. This is a favored language of demons due to its being the spoken language of most of the Jews of Galilee during the life of Christ, who himself spoke it. The demonic love of perversion extends to their use of the language spoken by the son of God—or, as Jefferson would have it, the rebellious rabbi who wielded his faith like a sword against the tyranny of the Romans. Either suits me.

Once I understood the language—and here Abigail rolled her eyes and said, "Of course you speak Aramaic"—I could hear that Jennifer was saying *Ancitif cannot be defeated.*

Ancitif. Once we puzzled out the syllables of that name, we tried various spellings in this omniscient index known as Google—and we located the story of the possession of the nuns of Louviers, more than three hundred years ago. A nunnery there came under the sway of lustful demons possessing the vicar and director. They beguiled the young nuns into a number of orgiastic

ANTICIF

INFERNUM CONJICIUNTUR

practices—and, it is alleged, ritual murders as well—before one of the nuns was overburdened by her guilt and leveled accusations at the two men responsible. These, Vicar Thomas Boulle and director Mathurin Picard, were duly charged. The name of the demon said to have masterminded these actions was Ancitif. Picard died before the trial, under unknown (but, one suspects, unnatural) circumstances. Father Boulle met his end at the stake.

The nun, Sister Barbara, who broke Ancitif's hold and made the accusations, was said to be freed by sacred lanterns from the cathedral adjacent to the nunnery. When I saw these lanterns, I recognized one of them! It was in Benjamin Franklin's possession when I visited Franklin in his house at Passy, in France, in late 1778. I was there as a courier for General Washington, charged with returning certain documents to Washington. I remember the lantern well, and remembered too that Franklin had given one to a chosen delegate from each of the colonies. Jennifer broke into my reverie to announce that she too had seen one of them, and knew where we could procure it.

We are going to get that lantern now.

Much has happened. We did indeed collect one of the Louviers lanterns, from a family called Weaver that appears to be part of a lively subculture of apocalyptic maniacs in the United States of 2013. Colloquially they are known as "preppers," for their obsessive focus on preparing for the End of Days—whether by nuclear means or demonic action, or simply through the (in their view) inevitable collapse of an immoral civilization. It was such a family, the Weavers, who possessed one of the sacred lanterns of Louviers. Apparently part of their "prepper" regimen includes the collecting of occult artifacts for use in whatever version of the end of the world they might encounter. Their house was a fortification as much as a dwelling place, ringed with traps and alarms; the Weavers themselves were as heavily armed as Abigail's officers—perhaps more so—and all too willing to use their weapons. Oddly, it seems those most deeply invested in the idea of the end of the world are also those who yearn for a pretext to perpetrate violence.

I, who know the real dangers of the End of Days, feel quite differently about violence. I am no shirker of what is necessary, but neither am I given over to bloodthirstiness or latent sadism. I am a warrior, a Witness. People such as the Weavers mean well, perhaps, but their fear curdles their good intentions, and endangers us all.

Jennifer knew them, and had participated in paramilitary training with them, but that made no difference in their demeanor when they caught Abigail and me coming out of their compound with the Louviers lantern. Guns were drawn and leveled, and only Jennifer's forceful presence allowed us to escape without bloodshed.

While we were thus occupied, however, the demon Ancitif was riding one of Captain Irving's officers into the very safe house where Irving thought to protect his family. There it killed Father Boland and forced Irving to go to the archives and give it General Washington's Bible. By the time we had disentangled ourselves from the Weavers, Irving and the demon-haunted Macey were already there. Had we not anticipated subterfuge on the part of the demon Ancitif, our cause might have been fatally set back— yet anticipate we had. I had removed the Bible from the archive ahead of time, and we also had enough time to prepare an ambush. I observed from a hiding place in the mouth of one of the tunnels leading away from the archive as Ancitif taunted Irving for his inability to keep his family safe. Irving bore this abuse, and further, he refused to tell Ancitif the locations of the Witnesses, information the demon desired most fervently. Little did Ancitif know that both Witnesses were within earshot at that moment, and preparing to announce themselves.

Miss Jenny once again was invaluable. She made herself a target of the demon's attention, and with incredible force of will prevented Ancitif from possessing her once again. Her diversion saved the life of Macey's mother, whom the demon was preparing to kill; once its attention was fully focused on its former host, we were able to maneuver it into an incomplete salt ring. As it raged, I leapt from my place of concealment and completed the ring, trapping the demon within. Repelled by the salt, which all demons hate, Ancitif could do naught but shower us with the most horrible invective as I began the recitation of the exorcism. Empowered by the Louviers lantern, the ritual froze Macey's demonic form in place and expelled the demon, with awful curses and screams of rage.

We have returned Irving and his family to their home. Macey has no memory of her possession, which is just as well. I fear, however, that there will be effects on her mother, which may not reveal themselves fully for some time. Knowing your child is possessed must be terrible enough; experiencing the infernally strong grasp of that child's hands around your throat surely must leave scars invisible to the eye.

We fear our children, and sometimes with good reason, for it is through their actions that we understand our failures. I see this only at a distance, for I had no effect on Jeremy—save by my absence, which is the signal failure of any loving parent.

For now, it is time to sit and gather my thoughts before Abigail arrives. We have developed a habit of convening in the aftermath of an event like this one just past, perhaps to share a glass of wine, perhaps only to share confidences. (The wine, I must say, is superb, far superior to the swill common in my day—although nothing matches a fine Madeira, a bottle of which was opened to toast the signing of the Declaration of Independence. In any event, I am heartily glad that the temperance movements that surged through the colonies have not persisted. The pleasure of a libation—in moderation, of course!—should be denied to no man or woman.)

I enjoy these conversations over drinks, and I have come to care deeply about Abigail. I am distant from all that I know, save for the irruptions of my previous life into this present, and those only serve to undermine my ability to acclimate myself to life in this maddening, astounding twenty-first century. Speaking with Abigail, simple talk between friends, is the best—perhaps the only—medicine with any therapeutic value against my peculiar malady.

The revelation of Jennifer's secrets has caused me to wonder whether the same might be true of Abigail. There is no evidence to suggest that she has suffered bouts of possession, but that is not the only means by which a demon may work through an unknowing human. Apart from her recollection of seeing the four trees and Moloch, Abigail's memories of her three days lost in the forest are gone, either erased or suppressed. She feels she should remember, however, and this feeling—together with her terrified renunciation of the experience in front of Jennifer—has transformed into an unbearable burden of guilt and denial; Jennifer, in contrast, embraced the vision. She opened herself to the reality of the demonic realms, and then her betrayal by her sister damaged her badly enough to render her vulnerable to Ancitif—and perhaps other demons as well? We do not know. Neither of them has the equilibrium one must possess to fight an enemy as wily and without compunction as our demonic adversaries. Both took up arms, which I find quite interesting—as if they knew that they were to be pressed into service in a war. Abigail chose legal means, Jennifer the route of the rebellious freedom fighter and soldier of fortune; yet both have arrived with hard-earned skills that will serve us well in the future. One hopes they will be able to resolve whatever barriers still lie between them.

LARGEST AMERICAN CITIES THEN AND NOW

Philadelphia 30,000
New York 25,000
Boston 16,000
Charleston 12,000

New York 8 million
Los Angeles 4 million
Chicago 3 million
Houston 2 million

[January 6]

Dream last night: I sat at supper with my father and my son. Neither spoke. On the wall, looming over the table, a portrait of General Washington. There was an empty chair at the table. The centerpiece was an enormous platter on which sat a whole roasted calf. All of us held knives, but none was willing to make the first cut.

———————————

My gift of eidetic—or "photographic," I must remember to say, since the word eidetic is not commonly known; I have only recently learned it myself—memory is, I fear, somewhat less impressive in an age when everything is on videotape, a technological wonder in and of itself, now superannuated by digital storage. I try to learn this age's methods of speaking, its jargon, even its rhythms. As I look back over these pages, do I already detect changes in the natural patterns of my syntax, learned and cultivated for three decades of life in the eighteenth century? Is a few weeks enough to effect such a change?

Totally.

That caused me physical pain.

———————————

I am sorry for Father Boland's death. He knew the tricks of the old demonologists, but was betrayed by that old bugbear, human error. I am intrigued that he knew of the protective qualities of salt. What is the old saying? "The Devil liketh no salt in his meat"? Like other folkloric truisms, this one is rooted in lost knowledge—in this case, salt's strong repulsion of demonic entities. For salt is eternal and incorruptible; it preserves what it touches, as with salted meats; it is the alchemical antithesis of the corruption and fickleness at the heart of demonic being. Father Boland knew this, and laid lines of salt around the safe house. However, when we had a chance to look over the scene, I noted that someone had interrupted the salt barrier across the threshold of the front door. This must have been an accident, as the demonically possessed officer would have been unable to touch the salt, or by any action cause it to be moved. A terrible misfortune, and one that cost lives—also a lesson in the dire consequences of even the smallest errors in this war we fight.

———

Abigail has recovered General Washington's Bible from its hiding place here at the cabin. I again notice a pungent smell about the book—a thoroughly nauseating stench, if I am to be honest—and I believe I now recognize it.

(Abigail's pithy assessment: "Smells like one of the pigs Jesus put those demons into.")

One of the pillars of eighteenth-century spycraft, as in any other age, was the transmission of hidden messages. The liquid obtained from the crushed and strained bodies of a certain species of glowworm makes a superb invisible ink—save for the unfortunate odor it begins to emit as the natural processes of decay occur within the molecules of the liquid. It is this smell that emanates from the pages of General Washington's Bible.

There is a message here.

December 18, 1799. That is the date written in the glowworm extract; it is written in General Washington's hand, which I know as well as I know my own; and it is four days after his death, when he was no longer general but president—or, more correctly, ex-president, having handed executive authority to his successor Adams.

Did George Washington write in this Bible after his death? One is tempted to employ the principle of Occam's razor, that the simplest explanation is the best—and that would lead to the conclusion that Washington was simply noting the future date to remind himself of an event or obligation. However, if I have learned into prison, that ye may be tried; and ye shall have tribulation ten days: be thou faithful unto death, and I will give thee a crown of life.

11 He that hath an ear, let him hear what the Spirit saith unto the churches; He that overcometh shall not be hurt of the second i death.

12 And to the angel of the church in Perga- mos write These things saith he which hath the sharp sword with two edges;

13 I know thy works, and where thou dwell- est, even where Satan's seat is and thou holdest fast my name, and hast not denied my faith, even in those days wherein Antipas was my faithful martyr, who was slain among you, where Satan dwelleth:

14 But I have a few things against thee, because thou hast there them that hold the doc trine of Balaam, who taught Balac to cast a stumbling- block before the children of Israel, to eat things sacrificed unto idols, and to commit fornication.

15 So hast thou also them that hold the doc trine of the Nicolaitanes, which thing I hate.

16 Repent; or else I will come unto thee quickly, and " will fight against them with the sword of my mouth.

17 He ' that hath an ear, let him hear what the

Spirit saith unto the churches; To him that overcometh will I give to eat of the hidden 1 manna, and will give him a white stone, and in the stone a new name written, which no man knoweth saving he that receiveth it.

18 And unto the angel of the church in Thy atira write; These things saith the Son of God, who hath his eyes ' like unto a flame of fire, and his feet are like fine brass;

19 I know thy works, and charity, and ser vice, and faith, and thy patience, and thy works; and the last to be more than the first.

20 Notwithstanding I have a few things against thee, because thou sufferest that wo man Jezebel, which calleth herself a pro phetess, to teach and to seduce my servants to commit fornication, and to eat tilings sacri ficed unto idols.

21 And I gave her space to repent of her fornica- tion and she repented not.

22 Behold, I i will cast her into a bed, and them that commit adultery with her into great tribula- tion, except they repent of their deeds.

23 And I-will kill her children with death; and all the churches shall know that I am he which searcheth the reins and hearts : and

A. M. cJr. 4100.	
Ro.18.28 Ep.3.3	
A. M. cJr. 4100.	
Ro.18.28 Ep.3.3	
A. M. cJr. 4100.	
Ro.18.28 Ep.3.3	
A. M. cJr. 4100.	
Ro.18.28 Ep.3.3	
A. M. cJr. 4100.	
Ro.18.28 Ep.3.3	

truly relish the heavenly manna ; nor can any such claim that evidence and assurance of his salvation, which is implied in the white stone and the new name here referred to. The church of Thyatira seems to have much resembled that of Pergamos, There were among them many eminent for good work-*, and charity, and faith, &c. but there was a gt bel among them. Some wicked woman, possibly of rank and influence, who, under he mask of a Christian profession, cou tenanced occasional attendance at idol temples did not see any great harm in those common aberations from purity and strict nds, which the world covers with the name of "juvenile indiscretions." We are uired, however, to "avoid all appearance of evil," and to ' hale (even) the garment ot ted by the flesh." The earliest, and some of the best modern commentators, indeed, consider this Jezebel not to have been a mere indi vidual, but an heretical party which d crept into the church (similar to the Nicolaitanes at Pergamos, and perhaps with ome female Nicolaitan at their head,) who pleaded for occa sional conformity to their agan neighbours. They admired architecture and statuary, ana there could be no harm see ing an idol temple. They loved music, and where could they hear it in such rfection as there? They were men of taste too, and where could their taste be so highly ratified wuh the richest viands and the cholrest wines ? Or they wished to cultivate good fellowship with their neighbours, and to oblige their kindred and friends : and what so likely to do this, as oc casionally associating with them in their devotions, hough they might not worship the idols in their hearts ? And, besides, (might these omplaisant Christians say,) Perhaps they may be induced to attend at our churches in turn, and who Knows but they may be converted?" These, and a thousand other ausible excuses might be made by these Jezebel professors, to cover or to excuse their as. But what says he, whose "eyes are like a flame of fire?" I wilt cast her into a bed, ad them that commit adultery with her.' But this is not a bed of ease, much less of leasure, but a bed of' great tribulation.'" and those who have lan

guished, or even seen others languishing, in bed, with the gout, ill-1 stone, and other acute diseases, must know what ' great tribulation" means. " And I will kill her children with death" — perhop* pestilence ', for Paul has inti'ht us, that sickness and death are often the consequence of spiritual degeneracy — ' For this cause many are weak and sickly among you, and many sleep.' (I Cor. xi. 30.) Have any of us been visited with personal or family sickness? It may then be well to in quire, has our conduct given no provocation for it? When the affections of a Christian are drawn from religion to the world, the mercy of God often sends affliction to bring him back again. And if any of our family idols have been taken from us, it is not only our duty to submit, (for that we must do,) but also to return to the only object whom we can love without the dan ger of excess. He "whose eyes are us a flame of fire,' may kill our children," to save both their souls and ours. We shall never know all the advantages of our afflictions in the present state: and wo unto those who are spared in this life, to be punished in another ! But some of these members of the church of Thyatira were, it seems, so little sensible of their degeneracy, that they boast ed of their attainments : they ' understood all mysteries.' as Paul saith, (1 Cor. xiii. 2,) but "had not charity ;" they boast ed of their acquaintance with ' the deep things of God, which they perverted and abused to the " depths of Satan.' The sect of Gnostics (o? knowing ones, as the word means) is not yet extinct ; and we have seen, with timely pain, the pleasure which "such persons take in supporting themselves wiser than their fellow Christians— that is, generally, in being "wise above what is written.' It is not, however, speculation, but faith and obedience only, that can gain the victory, but be that overcometh shall be exalted to a throne, and to a kingdom, like his Lord and Master. CHAP. III. Ver 1 – 13. Epistles to the churches of Sardis and Philadelphia. – Sardis was the ancient seat of Croesus and the Lydian kings, but is now - beggarly village, called Sart, in whose seven Christians only were counted a Tew years ago, and they were not allowed to build a church on the site anything in the course of my battle with the minions of Moloch, it is this: Demons care not a fig for Occam's razor.

This date is a clue. It must lead somewhere, and I must find out where. If General Washington meant this Bible to find its way into my possession then I suspect this clue was meant for me. After all, General Washington was a perspicacious man, and would surely have made arrangements for his soldiers to continue to fight in the event he did not survive to see the successful prosecution of the war against Moloch.

And, as he made clear to me, I was one of those soldiers—by which, I now understand, he meant I was a Witness. Why he never told me as much himself is a mystery I have not yet been able to unravel.

———————

Shortly before I fell to the Horseman's axe, I spoke to General Washington. This was in July 1781, shortly after Comte de Rochambeau had arrived in White Plains with French reinforcements the exhausted Continental Army desperately needed. Washington wished to attack New York, but Rochambeau dissuaded him, arguing that a strike at General Cornwallis in Virginia was both more feasible and in the end more decisive—for to dislodge Cornwallis would cripple the British and isolate their remaining forces in the north. At length Washington agreed. Before he left with the combined Franco-American force (which I have since learned won a great victory at Yorktown!), he wished for a private consultation with me.

We met in a house on the banks of the Bronx River. The army was to begin its march in the morning, but before their departure Washington wished to give me a most grave commission. Crane, he said. It is destiny that has brought you to America, and that destiny calls for you to play a pivotal role in the war that is to come. By that he meant not the Revolution, but the broader conflict of the forces of light against the legions of darkness.

I stand ready, General, said I; whatever task you set me, know that I will not rest until it is completed.

You have a gift, Washington said. You see through the human masks demons have learned to wear.

Of course, he referred to Tarleton. I know this now, but at the time I thought he was speaking figuratively. The nature of the gift to which he referred was unclear to me then. This was the first time General Washington had ever spoken openly of the work we did, the clandestine war that lay behind and underneath the Continental Army's battle for the independence of the colonies. In my naiveté I took him to mean spycraft; there is much I now see in a different light, and much I wish Washington had shared more openly, that I might have done him better service—and perhaps saved Katrina and Jeremy from what befell them.

Much of what we do—perhaps all of what we do—will be lost to history, he went on. You must not fight for glory, but for what is good and holy and right.

So I have endeavored to do, sir, I answered.

Remain here in New York, he said. Search out those among the redcoats a Hessian with the mark of a drawn bow. It may be a tattoo, it may be a scar. Find this man, for if you do not, he will lead a charge against us, and it will be such a charge that no army solely composed of men shall hope to resist it.

He detailed to me the forces he would leave in my command. Good men, seasoned veterans—Mohawk scouts and fighters as well. We were to hunt these men who bore the mark of the bow. Then it was time for him to rest before the march to Virginia began in the morning. Before we parted for the last time, however, he grasped my arm and offered these parting words:

Good will always rise.

We parted then, with those words in my mind—I recalled him saying the same thing once before, but more fully, during another meeting: *Good will always rise, like Lazarus from the grave.*

I did not take his words as prophecy at that time, but in retrospect I see them as such.

I have it. Lazarus. I must let Abigail know.

———

I have returned home to a most disturbing and mysterious note. While I do not recognize the sender, I have my suspicions about his identity . . .

MOLOCH SEES ALL

Damnable, this "autocorrect." I am convinced that the "text message" is an infernal conspiracy designed expressly to promulgate misunderstanding. Thrice I have messaged Abigail and each time this phone has changed my words. I spoke to the voice inside calling herself Siri, but she was no help. Perhaps my device is already obsolete; heaven knows obsolescence is built into everything these days.

What is happening to me? Am I now susceptible to envy regarding communications technology? The new clothes were the doorway, and I now stand on the threshold of absorption into the consumerist fantasia of this United States.

Nevertheless, I desire a newer telephone.

Poor Andy Brooks has presented himself to Abigail and poured out his heart. He loves her and wishes her to accept Moloch, that they two might be together during the End Times—and presumably in whatever hellish kingdom succeeds the war. She has of course refused.

How many of mankind's evil deeds are motivated by the curdling of love into obsession? True love consists not in possessing another, but in two minds, two hearts, meeting one another as equals, neither reaching to grasp yet both consenting to be held. One gives oneself in love; one cannot take another in love; for that is greed or lust going about in a debased masquerade of love.

Brooks, perhaps as a gesture of good faith to convince Abigail of the truth of his love, disclosed Moloch's reason for hunting General Washington's Bible. He desires not the book itself, but a clue held within it that will lead to the location of a map. The

anniversary (thirteenth, if we needed any more potential misfortune) of Abigail's encounter with Moloch looms, Monday next. He knows she is vulnerable around that date, as observance of it forces her to confront her actions—and inactions. None are so vulnerable to demons as those with a guilty conscience. She has forgiven herself, I think, as we discovered in the Valley of Death; but it is an ancient truism that forgiveness does not necessarily bring forgetting.

She rejected him, as she must. Even apart from his undead state and his allegiance to Moloch, she turned away his proposal for the homely human reason that she does not love him, and never has. Perhaps it would have been more expeditious for her to nurture his ambitions a little longer, but that level of subterfuge is not part of Abigail's personality. Only the direct route for her! It was the honest thing to do, and the correct thing; yet is has had its consequences. Brooks is lost to us, and will be our enemy henceforth. So let us see what we may find in General Washington's Bible about this map.

The Gospel of John, chapter 11. "Lazarus, come forth . . ." In General Washington's Bible there are ten extra verses, set immediately before Jesus calls out to God at verse 41—on a page clearly cut and glued into place well after the original book was printed and bound. I had thought the extra verses, which repeated the numbering 31-40, to be a code, but what emerged was another message, written in an invisible palimpsest over those ten verses. They were a marker rather than the message itself. I ardently pray for strength that I will be able to discharge this gravest of responsibilities and spare any other from the danger I now understand is mine to face.

December 18th, 1799

Instructions from President George Washington for Captain Ichabod Crane, Esquire.

Captain Crane:

If you are reading this missive, the War has resumed and your destiny to bear Witness been made manifest. Four days ago, I was diagnosed by Dr. William Thornton with a fatal case of croup and quinsy. Thornton tried to keep me alive by letting my blood, but I only grew weaker. As the end came, I drafted a plan.

I asked that my body be kept in state, preserved by Virginia's winter air, so that supernatural forces might aid me in a final mission.

Four days ago, I died. But through the arcane knowledge and cursed prayer beads of these occult forces . . .

I was resurrected.

And so my final mission was to skirt the icy bonds of Death and resurrect myself—a sin—but one I had to commit so that I could draft for you a map—a map charting the passage from Earth to Purgatory . . .

An indispensable weapon against the evils of War.

So it ends. There is a smear of ink on the page, from which one can extrapolate the eerie vision of George Washington, called briefly back to life and slumping to his death again, over the page on which this map and letter were drawn . . . Washington, a revenant! Inconceivable—and yet I see, and Abigail sees, the evidence, in Washington's own hand.

A map to Purgatory. With such a map I could find my own way to Katrina and bring her out. Moloch knows this.

Where is this map?

One notes that at the end of John 11, Jesus has gone into hiding. Is that part of General Washington's message? I think not. I must act decisively and quickly, for Moloch will not tarry.

———————

We have found a vital clue. The Reverend Josiah Knapp was one of the occult figures who participated in the brief resurrection of Washington. He must have been a powerful warlock indeed, to prolong his own life span so dramatically, until his recent end at the hands of the Horseman of Death, Abraham Van Brunt; but even though he is dead, we may yet be able to make use of his connection to Washington's ritual. His will requested that he be buried with his necklace of prayer beads—the same beads used as a focus of the necromantic energies of the ceremony. These will be laden with the sin inherent in reversing the natural cycle of life and death—and we are fortunate enough to have made the acquaintance of a man perfectly suited to interpret that sin and divine from it whether Knapp knew anything of the map's location: Henry Parish. We will meet him soon, at the cemetery, and indulge in one more bit of grave robbing.

———————

Henry Parish is an admirable man. The prayer beads were protected by a powerful hex that caused him great pain when he touched them, but he was not dissuaded—and now we have advanced another step in our mission to discover the location of the map to Purgatory.

Parish saw a vision of Josiah Knapp disembarking from a boat on a shoreline. Knapp and two other men were carrying something large. That was all he saw, but that may well be enough.

True wisdom is never lost, as the Masonic rites ensure its transmission. However, it is a dictum of the Freemasons that they must carry their individual secrets with them into death. This extends beyond those secrets carried in the mind, and includes objects of such particular importance that their possession must be strictly controlled. Such, I suspect, was George Washington's guiding principle—and Josiah Knapp's—when the arrangements for his burial were being made. The map must be with Washington, for Washington would have known the importance of making certain it did not fall into the wrong hands. The best way to do that would have been exactly what was done: Encode a message that only a very few trusted confidantes would have been able to discover.

There are two known tombs of Washington: in Mount Vernon, Virginia, and in the United States Capitol Building. Both are decoys. If Josiah Knapp carried Washington's body to an island in the Hudson River near Sleepy Hollow—which seems certain, for Sleepy Hollow is clearly the crucial battlefield of the war, and Josiah Knapp was the guardian of the secrets of that war—then the map will not be far from his tomb. Therefore, we must search the islands and discover Washington's real tomb before the minions of Moloch do.

I realize I have forgotten to mention that we were attacked in the cemetery by three of Moloch's monstrous acolytes, similar to the one we encountered in the tunnels while attempting to hold the Horseman prisoner—before I had learned of his true identity. Henry Parish was wounded by one, but insists he is well, and indeed demonstrates what must be a superhuman power of healing. Already the marks of the creature's claws are beginning to disappear from his arm. The only other being I have seen exhibit such healing is the Horseman; the powers possessed by a Sin Eater are greater than I would have suspected.

———

Abigail has strong misgivings about finding the map. She has raised the possibility that the reason for the protective hex on Knapp's prayer beads was that sometime after General Washington's (final) death, Knapp realized a new danger and took steps to prevent anyone from finding the map.

Abigail drives, and I write. (Aside: I believe she wants me to learn to drive, but it is difficult to know how serious she is, since her alternate proposal is, and I quote, "Or at least we could get you a horse and buggy so I don't have to chauffeur you around everywhere.") We are going to explore the islands of the Hudson. Another of Henry Parish's hard-won revelations sticks in the front of my mind: It was also the Reverend Knapp who conveyed Washington's Bible to Katrina so she could place it with my comatose body in the cave. I had suspected this but hesitated to believe it, because if he knew of the location of my body, that meant he protected that secret—and perhaps that was another reason for the Horseman to hunt him down. I am beginning to stagger under the weight of the lives lost to further our cause, and defend my life.

Also, if he feared the discovery of the map, why did he not return and remove it from the cave? There is a mystery here—another mystery, I should say—and we have not the clues to unravel it. My belief is that the hex on the beads was there to ward off Moloch and his minions. Why it should have so damaged Henry Parish is a puzzle that none of us understands.

Now is the time to cross a river. Surely General Washington would appreciate this symmetry. On Christmas night of 1776, he famously crossed the Delaware to raid a Hessian encampment at Trenton. Now we seek to raid his tomb to fight our Hessian enemies—some of whom, perhaps, were in Trenton when the Continentals took them by surprise? A good omen. Further, I am put in mind of both the proverbial crossing of Jordan and the mythological crossing of the Styx. In that context it seems quite fitting that we undertake this crossing in search of a dead man with whom we are hoping to speak—not verbally, but by means of what we find in his tomb.

———

John 11: 41. *Then they took away the stone from the place where the dead was laid.*

It was turning a stone that opened Washington's tomb. It sat alone in a clearing on Bannerman's Island, and bore the marks of human workmanship. For what purpose would a stone have been so placed? As a marker. Bannerman's Island is aptly named, for are we all not bannermen of the host of heaven? And it was there that we discovered what we needed to know . . . and also where we began to confront the problems that accompany the possession of such a powerful item as a map to Purgatory.

On the shore of Bannerman's Island, Abigail pried from Henry Parish the confirmation of what she had previously suspected: a prophecy from the Apocryphon of John, a book removed from the biblical canon in the early centuries after the

Crucifixion. This prophecy states that the two Witnesses would turn on each other when the Beast, surely Moloch, "rose from the Abyss," which just as surely refers to Moloch rising from Purgatory to oversee the final battle of the Apocalypse. She was quite skeptical of my assurances that we would treat the map as the immensely powerful and dangerous artifact it is. Before the tension between us could grow unmanageable I located the entrance to Washington's tomb and we entered. Was this another decoy? No, as the inscription IM—for Indispensable Man, a common moniker applied to Washington during the Revolution and thereafter—confirmed. We searched the crypt for the coffin that must surely be within, and found it by means of a secret keyhole in a statue of the Roman statesman Cincinnatus, grooved to match the Masonic ring I have worn since 1771.

CINCINNATUS

A leader in crisis, who yielded power the moment the crisis was past, and could not be persuaded to keep it for its own sake. He was notified that he had been nominated as dictator of Rome while he was plowing his field—a mere fifteen days later, after putting down the rebellion of the Aequians, he had resigned and was back at his plow. If absolute power corrupts absolutely, then Cincinnatus was truly an incorruptible man. Washington admired him. (The American city named for him, Cincinnati, was apparently known for its trade in pigs, and for hosting the first professional baseball team.)

It was too easy at that point. We had the map in our possession, and Katrina's freedom was within our grasp. That was when

Brooks, newly strengthened and utterly in the thrall of Moloch, collapsed the entrance to the crypt and attacked. It was only through the quick reaction of Henry Parish, who seized Brooks and consumed his sins, that he was prevented from killing us all—and even so, Parish's brave act only sufficed to give Abigail time to strike Brooks down with the pry bar we had brought to open Washington's coffin. I have never had to kill one who loved me, and by the grace of the Infinite (to use the preferred term of the deist) I never shall. I am filled with admiration that Abigail had the strength to act when to do otherwise would have doomed us all.

All Masonic structures are ideas given form in stone. Perhaps this is true of all structures—architects doubtless would say so—but it is an inherent feature of the works of Freemasons, and it was knowledge of this that saved our lives earlier today. For when Brooks revived—having already died, he could not be incapacitated for long by any physical means—we were able to trigger the crypt's lethal defenses, bringing its massive ceiling and pillars down on him while we made good our escape. We left not by the way we had come, for Brooks had sealed that entrance beyond our capability to excavate, but through the rear wall of the crypt's innermost sanctum. I knew there would be an exit therein, for it is another dictum of Masonic architecture that no structure of any importance be without a secret egress. Freemasons are ever conscious of the presence of their enemies.

Then came a difficult moment between Abigail and me. She knew Moloch needed the map to win the war, for without it he cannot prevent an incursion into Purgatory. That is his weakness. If we can strike into Purgatory, we can recover Katrina and thereby remove the hold Moloch maintains over the Horseman, Van Brunt. Abigail spoke of something else Brooks had said in addition to this, however: that the map also holds a secret that is key, not to the defense of Purgatory but to Moloch's strategy to prosecute and win his war against heaven. I know not what that secret may be; none of us does. But its existence terrified Abigail, as did her lingering fear of the prophecy that the two Witnesses will betray each other. She was utterly convinced that the map was the key to Moloch's victory—and could I place more importance on rescuing Katrina than on the very end of the world?

I could not.

I burned the map. It was the only way to halt that prophecy's self-fulfilling momentum and keep the trust Abigail and I have with each other, without which we have no hope. Abigail was becoming controlled by fear of this prophecy, and I by fear of her reaction to it. In the end it is the same fear, that we will not make our own decisions in the face of what seems such a powerful destiny. Moloch will not have the map. Abigail's concerns are somewhat assuaged.

I am alone again. Henry Parish has gone home. Abigail as well. Of Jennifer's whereabouts I know nothing, as usual.

Captain Irving is a better and stronger man than I had understood. He is attempting to shoulder the blame for a number of the deaths that have recently occurred. By doing so he protects his daughter, who remembers nothing of her possession by Ancitif. She would be shattered were she confronted with the knowledge that it was her hands (though Ancitif's will) that killed Father Boland and endangered her mother. This is not an especially heroic act in and of itself, for what father would not interpose himself between a daughter and the misguided force of the law? Irving's heroism is in his further duplicity, which encompasses several other deaths. He draws attention to himself as a suspect and thereby

frees Abigail and me to continue our work. Before long we will be forced to do something to protect him, but for now he is insulated—by his status and the loyalty officers of the constabulary command from one another—from the full consequences of his confession.

I occupy myself thinking of Katrina's necklace, the same one I selected on Van Brunt's behalf shortly before the disastrous end of his engagement to her. What became of it during the confrontation with Van Brunt in the tunnels I do not know, yet its memory is a talisman to me—of the promise I have made to help her escape, and of the dread menace of Moloch that stands between Katrina and me.

———————

I have a decision to make.

Abigail quoted the example of Cincinnatus, after seeing the sculpture of him in Washington's tomb. Indeed he provided a worthy template for how one must behave when in possession of power—that is, one must relinquish it the moment it is no longer necessary. Washington was emulating Cincinnatus when he rejected all pleas to continue as president, or even assume a more imperial role, and in this as in so many other things, Washington was the very model of good conduct. The memory of Cincinnatus was behind Abigail's insistence that we destroy the map. Of that I am certain. Perhaps it was too powerful to possess, and its true value lay in the damage we could do to Moloch's cause by destroying it. A saying popular in this time: Power corrupts, and absolute power corrupts absolutely. I reject it, although I understand its allure. I prefer a more recent saying, also familiar though regarded with less seriousness due to its source (and here I speak not of my impish contemporary Voltaire, but of a television figure, both spider and man, whom I encountered recently): With great power comes great responsibility.

———————

A few weeks ago, while under the sway of my melancholy at being torn away from my time and all I knew—in short, feeling quite sorry for myself—I attempted to discover what the great men of my time had accomplished during the years remaining to them after my interment. In light of recent events regarding General Washington, I am put in mind of correspondence between Benjamin Franklin and the eminent French scientist Jacques Barbeu-Dubourg. The two took up the question of whether it might in some future age be possible to lay the dead aside and awaken them by means of science, after careful preservation.

> *I wish it were possible . . . to invent a method of embalming drowned persons, in such a manner that they might be recalled to life at any period, however distant; for having a very ardent desire to see and observe the state of America a hundred years hence, I should prefer to an ordinary death being immersed with a few friends in a cask of Madeira, until that time, then to be recalled to life by the solar warmth of my dear country! But . . . in all probability, we live in a century too little advanced, and too near the infancy of science, to see such an art brought in our time to its perfection . . .*

'Twas not a cask of Madeira, but a mighty enchantment, that worked my long sleep and eventual revival—but I can appreciate the coincidence that Franklin speculated on this while events gathered themselves to hurtle toward the 232-year hiatus of my waking life. O, Franklin, most irritating yet clairvoyant of men—is there nothing you did not contemplate, or anticipate?

I was brought back to life for a reason.

Katrina, Katrina . . . I have seen the map. I know the way and will redraw it. Hold on a little longer.

[January 20]

There is to be an eclipse today. I believe I will go for a walk before the sun disappears, and collect my thoughts before meeting Abigail and plotting the next act in our war against Moloch. I hope she is bearing up well, as this is the anniversary of her encounter with him. I suspect he will have a commemoration planned. We must be vigilant.

SUPERSTITIONS REGARDING ECLIPSES

Eclipse, from Greek ἔκλειψις, *"abandonment"—one certainly hopes that there will be no literal abandonment today!*

Often held to be an omen of the coming death of a leader—or earthquake

Chinese: Dragon (or dog) eating the sun

Indian: Immerse oneself in water for protection—akin to baptism?

Muslim: Special eclipse prayer, Salaat ul-Kusoof

Mayan, Aztec: Causes birth defects; pregnant women must wear something red and protect themselves with an arrowhead

Aleut: Place all cooking and eating utensils upside down

This day, which began in such a delightful fashion, is rapidly disintegrating into chaos. But what else would one expect from a war for the souls of humanity?

And also—this morning as I walked in the forest, I encountered a woman dressed in clothing from the century of my birth. At first I took her to be Katrina, and believed myself to be in the grip of a vision of some sort. Upon further investigation, however, I learned that I had in fact come upon a reenactment (full of inaccuracies, but sincerely meant) of the battle between the Marquis de Montcalm's mercenaries and the Forty-second Highlanders. Of all the leisure pursuits one might enjoy . . . yet I must not judge. The woman I at first mistook for my wife was in fact a seamstress specializing in the creation of antique clothing for people whose hobby it is to put on masquerades of historical events. I will refrain from further comment on this practice, save to say that I am quite thrilled to have been able to purchase an entire wardrobe of new clothing.

Things, as I have heard others say, seemed to be looking up . . . until I was interrupted in my conversation with the lovely reenactor (I almost told her that I once romanced another seamstress, Betsy Ross, but bit my tongue before I could do something so foolish) by a call from Henry Parish. He arrived shortly after I returned to Corbin's cabin to find Abigail and Jennifer already there. Abigail bore the news that Captain Irving had signed a confession to the murders of Officer Jones and Father Boland. O brave dissembler! We must find a way to save him from his attempt to save us.

Henry, for his part, has had a premonition of Moloch in the forest against a background of four unnatural white trees. Abigail and Jennifer immediately recognized this as a feature of their encounter with the demon years ago. Continuing, Henry recounted the rest of the vision: a rider on a horse whose flesh was burned but not consumed, brandishing a sword.

Revelation 6:4. *And there went out another horse that was red: and power was given to him that sat thereon to take peace from the earth, and that they should kill one another: and there was given unto him a great sword.*

The Horseman of War.

Today is the day he is to be raised into this world, via the breaking of the second seal.

Abigail has gone to the precinct office to see if she might speak to Irving, who is not answering his phone. Astonishing what a transgression this has become, to refuse to be available to anyone at any moment. I am grateful to escape into this journal, and be alone with my thoughts, though it mean rudeness to Henry and

Jennifer, both of whom would draw me back out into their plan. We are to meet Abigail at the archive.

I have confessed to copying the map.

Abigail, to her credit, was angry but understood that my weakness has been converted by recent events into a strength. For we now know that Henry Parish's vision of the four trees marks the spot where Moloch will engineer the entry of the Second Horseman into this realm. The only way to prevent this is to magically shield that location, blocking the Horseman's emergence—and the only person we know who is capable of creating such a shield is Katrina. Therefore my reproduction of the map—a minor and necessary treachery—will be key to our survival. The Horseman of War rides up from the infernal dimensions, and we are charged to stop him. So we must.

I recalled to Abigail and the others what General Washington said to me: The battle for this world would be won or lost in a township that took its name from the hallowed ground on which it lay, a doorway between worlds.

Sleepy Hollow. The name is a corruption of the original, which meant to convey that this was the *hallowed* place where evil *sleeps,* and those dedicated to the light stand watch.

One must note here that Sleepy Hollow's current population is 144,000 souls—exactly the number to be saved according to the Doctrine of Election. This is the number of the saved in the seventh chapter of Revelation, and it is held to be the number of souls who bear the mark of Grace and will stave off the victory of evil during the Tribulation. This similarity can be no accident. It is yet one more symbolic indicator of the crux at which the battle between light and dark has arrived. The Tribulation is upon us.

To be spoken at the entrance:
We, the penitent, with humble heart
upon this threshold do summon thee
in mirror'd form appear,
a gateway to the world between worlds.

Hudson River

Surrounding woods

Surrounding woods

Village

Respectfully submitted
George Washington

The content of this map
said to change and supernatural
occurrence, it's only to be
in interaction by the one initiated

The map features a number of ley lines, some of which I did not recognize as such until I understood the peculiar key of Washington's undead cartography. (I feel certain that no man before me has ever written those three words in sequence.) These are lines of occult energy, tracking certain wellsprings and currents of power inherent in Earth itself. Their use is common in magical practices across the world. But where were these ley lines to be placed on a map? Sleepy Hollow, without a doubt, but where? I regarded maps of the town, and conjured a map of how it had appeared in 1781; I returned my attention to General Washington's map; and yes! There it was. I could see where Washington had marked out a particular bend in the river; how the suggestion of barrows on Washington's map appeared on the contemporary map too, as dogleg turns in roads where there appeared no reason for them.

The ley lines on the map intersect in a location deep in the forest on the edge of town—that is the portal to Purgatory.

Moloch's riddle still troubles me, however. *The saint's name is a sign. When you know my meaning, War will take form.*

This would seem to suggest that we should not learn the saint's name. Yet that cannot be the case, because if Moloch needed us to know the saint's name for War to arrive, he could simply tell us. Therefore we reason that this part of the riddle is at least as much threat as prophecy; that Moloch believes we will learn the name too late to prevent the profane annunciation of the Horseman of War.

Abigail has set Jennifer the task of listening to Sheriff Corbin's recordings, hundreds of hours of his musings and investigations as he sought to understand the arcane forces animating the history of Sleepy Hollow. She is a dogged and careful person, and I have no doubt she will find the answer if it is there.

For my part, I have found the doorway between worlds of which General Washington spoke, and now is the time to use it.

I must go into Purgatory and bring out my beloved. I will not be going alone; Abigail will be with me. (I told her of the meaning of the word *eclipse* and she—plucky, brave Abigail!—countered with, "Nobody abandons anyone today. That's for damn sure.") We two Witnesses will traverse the portal between this world and Purgatory. The incantation, inscribed at the edge of Washington's map, is beautiful in its simplicity:

We, the penitent, with humble heart upon this threshold do summon thee: in mirror'd form appear, a gateway to the world between worlds.

Purgatory. Entry is forbidden, and it tests those who come not by the road of death; to eat or drink of anything that is offered is to surrender one's soul in perpetuity. To forget the illusionary nature of the world presented—for nothing in Purgatory is real—is to become an illusion oneself, trapped behind the mirror until the end of time.

It is a bold move indeed, to go into such a place willingly. But what manner of soldier would I be were I not willing to risk my own life in the effort to preserve so many others? Apart from that, there is no death I would not face if it meant bringing Katrina out of Purgatory and into the light again. She is indispensable to our cause, for one; only she can work the enchantment to seal the portal against the coming of the second Horseman. Yet beyond that she is my wife, my beloved, mother of the son I shall never know— and if men of good heart will not face the horrors of hell for those they love, then love itself is doomed.

Like Orpheus I will descend, but my Eurydice will not look back.

These will not, I hope, be words of farewell to this journal—to which I have become quite attached—but the possibility must be acknowledged, since to enter Purgatory is to put oneself at the mercy of Moloch. That will be slim mercy indeed.

If I do not survive these next hours, someone else must continue the work we have begun. This journal will assist that person, I hope, whether it be Abigail, Henry Parish, or another party whose role in this shadowy war is yet to be revealed—although I hope much more fervently that I will return to this world, with Katrina, and have no need of a successor! A word to whoever might read this: Know that you might be called upon to perform great deeds. Know also that you need not be great beforehand to do so, for no hero began a hero, and all of us are proven by our actions.

Here endeth the advice. Time is short, and so will I be. I will write to calm myself a little, and clarify my thinking. Abigail too is preparing, and Henry; each of us, I think, is grateful for a private moment before we embark on an action of so fraught and uncertain an outcome.

Katrina. I would think only of you, but I also am thinking of the prophecy regarding Witnesses: that one of us will turn on the other and both will thereby perish. I am sure Abigail is thinking of it too. Not all prophecies must necessarily come true, for prophets are human and prone to the same errors as any other—yet I have seen enough in these past weeks to understand that there is an inspiration beyond the world of the senses. I fear that the words of the Apocryphon of John may yet come to bear. I would walk through the fires of hell itself to bring Katrina back, but surely Moloch knows of the prophecy of the Witnesses as well. He will seek to turn us against each other, for dividing friends is one of evil's surest methods for corrupting and destroying the good in humankind—"that they should kill one another." Abigail and I must be vigilant. What a pitiable circumstance, to be forced to think of one's closest ally as potentially one's mortal enemy.

I have, as they say in this age, been there before. With Abraham Van Brunt, certainly. Then, however, I had fewer allies in whom I felt complete trust. Now I have at least three: Abigail herself, Miss Jenny, and Henry Parish. Together we will find a way to confront Moloch, to force our way through the rigors and perils of Purgatory, and prevent the advent of the Horseman of War. Particularly I place my trust in Abigail, for in truth I am not the worthiest of the two Witnesses, but only the one who benefits from the exemplary actions of the other.

These past weeks would surely have been a descent into madness without the steadying presence of Abigail. I marvel at her equanimity, her loyalty, and—not least—her wit, which has done so much to keep the shock of this future from overwhelming me. They thought me fit for the asylum at first, and so I might have been, had she not made efforts to keep me on an even keel. Every man who falls into a magical slumber for two centuries and more should be so fortunate as to have a Lieutenant Abigail Mills awaiting him when he awakens. I could not have hoped for a better companion and fellow Witness. Abigail, if I do not return from Purgatory, and if you read these pages, know that I hold you in the highest esteem and that my affection and respect for you are boundless. I hope you teach me how to operate an automobile someday—but I fear your efforts to force me into contemporary dress were always doomed to fail.

Still, my mind returns to the 232 years that have passed since I saw my wife in this mortal realm. Only when I think about that amount of time do I feel the centuries, and it is still difficult to believe so much time has elapsed, rather than only a matter of several weeks—less, in fact, than some of our other separations, when I was on missions to the southern colonies, or once to Paris. More properly, it was Passy, as I have mentioned, the second time I met that gasbag Benjamin Franklin. In the six years Katrina and I were married, we spent perhaps a total of two years apart. That was not unusual then, when travel was so much more difficult—not for nothing did it develop from the same root as the word *travail*. Now . . . perhaps now we never need be apart again. Perhaps we shall live together in the twenty-first century as we intended to after Independence in the eighteenth. Then, we imagined what the year 1800 might bring . . . now?

What will she look like outside of Purgatory? I look exactly as I did in 1781, and there are a great many more mirrors here than there were then, so it is easy to keep minute track of one's physical appearance. An age of vanities, this one is.

One must be able to joke, even at moments most fraught and dangerous. Life is marvelous, and grand, and the moment one loses sight of this central truth, one has taken the perilous step into the shadow of despair . . . and that is exactly what Moloch desires. Martin Luther was legendary for breaking wind at the devil: "But I resist the devil, and often it is with a fart that I chase him away." Inspired by this example, I mock the devil's minions. Then, bolstered by laughter and comradely feeling, I kill them.

We are almost ready to enter Purgatory, and I must put this journal down. I look forward to picking it up again, and committing to words the experience of feeling my wife's hand in mine. I am resolute, yet I also confess to a creeping fear that another shoe is yet to drop. (This is another superb expression with which I have recently become acquainted.) For does *apocalypse* not mean a revealing, an unmasking of a truth heretofore unimagined—and perhaps unimaginable?

What truth could that be?

Henry is watching me, with a peculiar expression on his face. I believe he is more concerned than he would like to admit about the prospects of our attempt to penetrate Purgatory and liberate Katrina. I will not ask; he is entitled to keep his thoughts to himself, and I certainly need no more trepidation added to that which I already feel. Henry did not seem an emotional man during our first interactions, but unless I am badly misreading his face, he is feeling some manner of profound emotion. I cannot tell what; other than joy, emotions intensely felt are often indistinguishable to me.

Virtually everyone I have met since reawakening here in Sleepy Hollow has had a role to play in this first part of the war against Moloch. Now that we are about to strike our first decisive blow, I have a moment to think, and I return to an idea that has often recurred over these past weeks. If coincidence is God's way of remaining anonymous, He has surely signed His name to the events of these past weeks.

All of it rushes together in my mind. Awakening, the first automobile I saw (and very nearly the last, as it almost ran me down); meeting Abigail and beginning to understand the truly incomprehensible nature of what had happened—yes, one can understand that something is incomprehensible; in fact, one must if one is not to beat one's head against the wall mistaking it for a problem that can be solved. The creatures, one after another, converging on Sleepy Hollow as if they could sense the great magic and the great evil being mustered here. The piecemeal development of my intuition of Moloch's involvement, and the simultaneous discovery of Katrina's true nature and her plight. On and on! So much in a few weeks! And now we stand on the threshold of forcing back a dread enemy, and crippling our greatest adversary just when he thought victory at hand.

These are strange times indeed. Plastic and satellites and water bottles and NorthStar and women in trousers; machines to make coffee; telephones that speak; telephones! The language, faster and more aggressive than in my day. Strange times.

This is where the battle turns.

May the grace of the Almighty guide us. More anon.

I must also leave these pencil shadings of two scraps of paper I recently found in the binding of an edition of *Poor Richard's Almanack*. The book was among Sheriff Corbin's materials, in a file on Reverend Knapp, but I had not taken notice of it until recently. I paged through it, at times struck by Franklin's homespun wisdom and at other times barely able to restrain my irritation at his arrogance.

In any event, I discovered these scraps and noted that when held at an angle to the light, they manifested the impressions of letters. I found a pencil and shaded over the impressions, ever so lightly, and thus revealed:

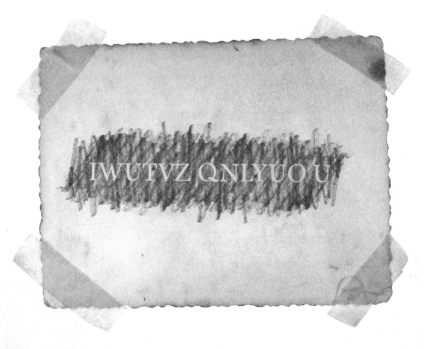

Either these shadings are nonsense, or more so-called Vigenère ciphers.

Given the Freemasons' love of these codes, I suspect the key is CICERO but have not had time to work through the decryption. Abigail calls. Will return to these soon.

JMNPWW TMEPLP

About the Author

Alex Irvine is the author of twenty-nine books, including the International Horror Guild, Locus, and Crawford Award–winning *A Scattering of Jades,* as well as the acclaimed near-future thriller *Buyout* and tie-in titles with *Supernatural, Transformers, Tintin, Pacific Rim,* and Marvel Comics (*Hellstorm, Son of Satan; Daredevil Noir; Iron Man: Rapture*). He holds a Ph.D. in English and was an English professor at the University of Maine for six years.

Follow Ichabod and Abbie
on their next adventure . . .